SHIN'AR, MY LOVE

SHIN'AR, MY LOVE

Love Amid the Ruins

MARTY DUNCAN ED.D.

**A Salute to the Survivors
Of an Ancient War**

The contents of this work including, but not limited to, the accuracy of events, people, and places depicted; opinions expressed; permission to use previously published materials included; and any advice given or actions advocated are solely the responsibility of the author, who assumes all liability for said work and indemnifies the publisher against any claims stemming from publication of the work.

This book is a work of fiction. Places, events and situations in this story are purely fictional. The history (portrayed in the background) is a shortened, condensed retelling of early Earth history founded in the work of several historians and archaeologists. All of the actual historical persons are long time dead.

The reader is invited to visit the author's website at www.martyduncan.us

Cover Image: Castle Romeo weapon test on Bikini Atoll 27 March 1954 Courtesy of United States Department of Energy [PD-USGov]

Library of Congress Control Number: 2016932293
Pilot's Mate, The , Saint Peter, MN
Publisher: O'magadh Media, Saint Peter, Minnesota. USA

ISBN: 0692632190
ISBN 13: 9780692632192

FORWARD

The novel '*Shin'ar My Love*' presents an alternative paradigm of history founded in the work of Zacharia Sitchen, Graham Hancock and Robert Schoch. The landing station on Mars actually existed. The underwater large constructions actually exist in our oceans. The Anunnaki Rebellion that resulted in the creation of *Homo sapiens* actually happened.

With Appreciation of the hundreds of archeologists, historians and translators of Sumerian, Akkadian, Chaldean, Hebrew, and Hittite cuneiform tablets, *please remember* this novel is fiction. The novel is a salute to all those translators.

The old myths frequently referred to an ancient, highly technological global civilization that was destroyed twice by a worldwide cataclysm sometime in the prehistory of today's world. This novel takes place during the Eleventh Dynasty of Egypt and the Age of Sumer (also called Shin'ar) and Akkadia (ie. 2050 B.C. to 2000 B.C.)

The symbol ✗ represents the 'Star' symbol used in Sumerian cuneiform to indicate names of Anunnaki lords, thus ✗Anu, ✗En.Lil, and ✗En.ki etc.

Arya, Aryan

"An Arya is one who hails from a noble family, of gentle behavior and demeanor, good-natured and of righteous conduct."

Amarakosa (a Sanskrit Lexicon)

Anunnaki, Anunnaki Lords

The Anunnaki Lords came to Earth from Nibiru, with the intent of mining gold in South Africa and Peru. When their sons rebelled, they used their sciences to create a new race of slaves, the ancestors of *homo sapiens*.

Anunnaki Rank (the Council of 12)

60 Anu (King on Nibiru)	55 Antu (His spouse)
50 Enlil (Lord on Earth)	45 Ninlil
40 Enki (also Ea)	35 Ninki
30 Nanna / Sin (Nan.Nar)	25 Ningal
20 Uta / Shamash	15 Inanna / Ishtar
10 Ishkur / Adad	5 Ninḫarsag

Anu Naki: 'Ant Friends' (Hopi Mythology)

The 'Anu Naki' saved the Hopi people *First* from Fire, then *Secondly* from Water disasters.

Mohenjo-Daro (a Capitol City in the Indus Valley)

"...white hot smoke rose in infinite brilliance and reduced the city to ashes ...and people grew boils on their skin and hair fell out."

The *Mahabharata* of India

PROLOG

"Your people . . .you will lead. Much sorrow . . .you will see. Much joy . . .in a new child's first cry." The blind old woman touched the girl's face. "Your face . . .I see . . .looking at a great black cloud filled with anger, red with vengeance."

The little girl watched as the old haggard woman called Málóid by the village children pulled her hand away. A tear formed in the girl's eye. There was a muffled sound from inside the girl. The old woman turned her head to listen. Her eyes were sightless, cloudy with gray matter. Her gray hair straggled to her shoulder. She wore an old coat of faded leather that reached to her feet. She sat with her feet on the bottom step. Behind her an enormous pier stretched along the shore. It was the meeting place; once the place of fishing boats.

The little girl watched the old woman's hands come to her shoulders and move down. The woman's gnarly hands felt the puffy sleeves of the girl's dress.

"I know you will lead. What color is your dress?" she asked.

"Yellow."

"You are not afraid?"

The girl looked down at the woman's bare feet. "A little."

"Remember my words. You will lead. You will see a great black cloud."

"Yes, Málóid, I will remember."

"What is your name, child?"

"Say-leest-ay" my mother says. She spells it *C-e-l-i-s-t-e."*

Celiste turned away from the wooden pier and the old woman. She walked up the sandy slope toward their village, a collection of small houses and animal pens built on the edge of the Euphrates River that stretched to the north. She was expected to return quickly. A soft breeze scattered her unruly hair. She looked up and saw her 'new' father Mica working with his men. They were building a platform for Lord Enki's temple.

Celiste would remember the words of the village seer. She would also remember this day. She could not know that someday she would be asked to lead a squad of women and to rebuild an abandoned village.

Celiste joined her new mother Misha at the door of their house. They were indeed fortunate. Mica's rank as Supervisor gave him certain privileges, which included a house with four rooms, a pen for sheep and goats and a fenced plot of land for vegetables. Misha was slim, a willowy woman with tracks of age at the corners of her eyes. She wore her long white robe over a tunic of sky blue. Her black hair implied she was of the Aryan race; Celiste's hair had slowly faded to light brown.

There were comments around their village. The new girl at Mica's house could not possibly be of the blood line of Lord ✗Enki. His hair was jet black; his half-sister's hair was black also. The young girl they called '*Say-leest-aye*' could not be of the royal family. Yet, as Mica had said, "We met the Lord, her father. His hair is black. Her grandmother ✗Ningal has rank 25 on the Council of Twelve. Celiste will have the same rank when she is grown."

When Misha was asked about Celiste's mother, she responded, "I was told to say, 'She has been exiled for improper behavior'." When asked what constituted improper behavior all Misha could do was raise an eyebrow and shrug.

Misha and Celiste turned to the north where they saw Mica on a raised platform, shouting directions to his men. He wore his best coat over a light yellow shirt in a material they called cotton. Mica's best coat of pale leather had been cleaned and stretched by a friend. His face was newly scraped and his hair slicked back with an oil of desert palm. His role this day was to meet Lord ✗Enki as he approached and lead his train of guards to the new platform.

From the south came a squad of men armed with lances and swords. The small group of eight men was followed by Lord ✗Enki, walking slowly while he talked with his Vizier. ✗Enki wore a long white robe. His black hair was shiny and framed his face. His straight nose and high cheekbones seemed to make his face longer than most. He was a full head taller than his Vizier; and two heads taller than his guards. He was followed by four men carrying poles on which was stretched a red banner. Their lord walked in the shade created by the banner.

Celiste pointed at the guards and said, "Short?"

"Yes, that is the word."

"Why?"

"They are Beag, the slaves of Lord ӾEnki. They come from a land far away."

"Why?"

"Because they do. They were born to work in the mines," she added.

"They look strong. Is that the word?"

"Yes. But you cannot trust them. They are dangerous."

"Does Mica trust them?"

"You are very smart for one so young. Yes, he says he shows them how to cut stone and they 'grab' how to do it quickly."

"They have mates?"

"Their mates work in the fields where we grow barley, wheat, radishes and the long tube some call 'Cumberly'," said Misha.

Celiste was left to ponder this observation. She knew everyone in their village worked at some task each day. She knew the Lord was pleased with all the work that was done each day. His household women would come and gather vegetables and perhaps they would honor a house by selecting a small sheep for the Lord's table.

The procession passed by the last of the houses and approached the slope up to the temple. The temple was being re-built on the foundation of an older temple that was submerged during a flood.

Celiste saw her new father Mica jump from the platform and approach the symbol of power in their village. When he was fifteen feet from ӾEnki he began to bow, once then twice. When he began to bow a third time Lord ӾEnki reached out and touched his shoulder and said something. An enormous smile formed on Mica's face.

Celiste looked up at her new mother Misha and said, "I hope someday I can impress this Lord. I want to work with Mica."

Misha smiled down at her and said, "Someday."

Chapter 1

Gray clouds spread across the heavens. An occasional hawk could be seen turning in the wind, a flash of white feathers against the indistinct slowly moving clouds. The sun was above the horizon; an area of clouds was lightly lit in orange. Celi stood near her tent and rubbed her arms against the early morning chill. She wondered if the distant hawk was a premonition of evil events to come. She could not know her life would take a twist. This day would lead her to be a witness of the sudden, blistering death of two cities.

Nor could she know this day would bring the slow painful death of a worker in her grandfather's squad of stone workers.

Behind Celi she heard a soft groan; it was more of a mumble from her grandfather Mica. His ancient back complained when he began to rise from his sleeping platform. She stepped back inside her tent to the small table that held her wash basin. Her hands plunged into the cold water; she splashed her face. She tried to rub the sleep out of her eyes. She used an old thread-bare towel on her face; a second groan told her Mica was on his feet.

She hung the towel over the wooden rod that was suspended from two ropes. With her right hand she smoothed her cotton tunic and stretched it across her chest. Her left hand brought the front of the tunic across the right. She proceeded to fold the left edge under to form a 'v' at her neck. Then she took her wide belt and wrapped it around her middle and tied it at her hip. She reached up and flicked water out of her hair; she twisted her hair into a bun and held it. With her other hand she wrapped her hair inside a wide decorated wrap that would protect her hair during the work day.

As he passed her Mica patted her shoulder and said, "Another day…"

"…to work for our Lord Enki." She finished the daily mantra.

Mica smiled while he rubbed his lower back. He was proud of his granddaughter. She was a head taller than his workers; her straight nose and flat forehead proclaimed her descent from the Lords of the land. Her light brown hair turned white when lit by reflected sun off the river. When she smiled the deep, deep blue of her eyes could cause a man to become shaky in the knees. Yet it was her eyes and her hair that raised a question: how could she be descended from the Lords who had black hair and black eyes that would haunt the minds of those who saw them?

Mica had long ago learned not to raise such questions. Celi came to live with him when she was four-years-old. He was informed by 'decree' written on papyrus that Celi was a granddaughter of Ningal, a princess on the Council. In no uncertain terms it was explained to him that his role was to raise her to be strong and determined. Mica had no children. He and his mate Misha were proud of their little girl. They watched as she learned to rebuke those who tried to chastise her for her light brown hair.

"Those boys said I am not of Lord Enki's family," she told Mica one day.

"You are not," said Mica, "of this Lord's family."

"No?" said Celi quietly.

Tears began to well up in her eyes.

"Your family lives in a royal temple in Nippur. Many days travel from here."

"Have you seen them?"

"Once, long ago. When you were knee high."

"What did you see? ...Oh, brave grandfather?"

"They brought me into a large hall with tapestries hung on the walls. It was there I met the Lady Ningal, your grandmother."

"Tell me..."

"The Lady is tall. She is one-half head taller than your grandfather," said Misha.

"And she asked you to take me away from her?"

"Yes. She gave me a papyrus with a decree. And a silver medallion."

Mica opened a small cloth bag and showed Celi the medallion. It was a silver star of six points inside a thick silver ring. The outer ring held six dark green gem stones. "From a far land, 'where riseth the sun,' she told me."

Celi watched her ancient grandfather as he stepped from their tent. She knew he missed 'his Misha' as he called her. Celi loved her Misha and often remembered the 'Mid-summer's day' when she heard Misha had gone to the Heavens.

Her right hand came up. She touched her medallion; the same she received six years in the past when she was twelve. It was her badge of rank; her badge that declared her descent from people she had not met.

Her people were the 'Lords,' what some called 'royal' and some called Aryan. Celi, however, had come to accept her role in life was to help her 'grandfather' Mica and help to rebuild their city, Eridu. [End Note 1]

Celi and Mica walked up the path through a grove of date palms. Their route went up the sides of an old mound. She walked slightly behind her revered grandfather. As they walked they discussed the day's work. Mica's troop of stone workers were about to finish the high walls of the main chamber inside the temple. Their task was to rebuild the Temple in Eridu, near the river called Euphrates. The temple had been buried in sand and mud during a flood 800 years in the past, as Mica explained it. His workmen were rebuilding a new temple, larger and taller, upon the foundation stones of the old temple. Mica saw several men climbing the scaffolding on the outside of the temple and wondered why they hurried.

Celi and Mica left the grove of date palms at the base of the mound. They were ancient, perhaps from before the flood. Above the palms stood three Joshua trees, bare and spindly with bent trunks. Mica walked a wide circle around the three. He believed Joshua trees represented the ghosts of warriors who died in battle. Mica asked but Lord Enki would not allow him to cut them down.

The mound held the remains of three or four earlier temples. On the top were four platforms, each as tall as a man. The second platform was smaller than the lower platform and so on for four platforms. A stairway led to the level upon which the temple itself was being built. To the left of the massive tall entry there stood a carved relief of a man perhaps sixteen feet tall with a cone hat upon his head. He held a bow in one hand with a sheath of arrows on his back. To the right of the entry an enormous bull with forward pointing horns served to remind those who entered that the lord of the land provided all that was good in their lives. The bull was a symbol of fertility. Above the door was carved a disc with wings, the symbol of the divinity of the Lord Enki. It was to be his temple.

When Mica and Celi entered the temple hall they saw four men with swords at their hips. The men wore the red tunics of royalty and held four poles. A tent was suspended from the four poles. Underneath on an elevated chair sat their Lord, Enki. He raised a hand to bring Mica toward him.

"I come. To watch the sunrise outside my temple," said the Lord without a comment about the clouds that covered the heavens.

Mica bowed low toward Lord Enki. Celi echoed Mica's action.

"Yes, my Lord," said Mica with deference.

"Does the work proceed?"

"Yes, my Lord."

"And the work?"

"Every day except the twelfth day. We thank our Lord for the extra rations."

"Did your men like the beer?"

"My Lord should feel gratified. They drank it all."

"Of nature, all men." Enki smiled. "This woman, there. Is she sweeping ash from a fire?"

"Yes, my Lord." Mica saw the old woman; she was bent from years in the mines. He saw her use a bunch of reeds to sweep the white marble floor. Mica did not choose to tell Lord Enki that he forbade the men to drink the beer until after the end of the work day. They celebrated with a fire.

"Do not permit fires. Not inside my temple."

Mica bowed to indicate he understood.

"The fire leaves a scar on this beautiful white stone."

Mica nodded to indicate he accepted the ruling of his Lord.

Enki nodded toward Celi. "This woman?"

"Is Celi, granddaughter of Ningal of Nippur." [EndNote 2]

Enki beckoned her. As she approached she clearly saw the deep lines in his face and the thinning hair that was once black. The skin under his chin sagged. There were spots on the backs of his hands. He wore a short tunic and she saw deep blue veins in his legs.

Celi bowed her head in respect. She looked up into his eyes and saw they were deep black, the blackest she had ever seen.

"Celi, granddaughter of Ningal, you help Mica? …I am told?"

"Yes, my Lord."

"I am told …when Mica was sick you worked with his men and gave them directions, told them how to connect the stones of the wall?"

"Yes, my Lord." She bowed in respect.

Enki smiled. He mumbled something that sounded like 'war and building are for the young.' He looked around and waved at his Captain who stood in the shade cast by the temple wall. The Captain said "Go" to four men who stood nearby. The four, armed with scabbards and short swords, ran up. The moment Enki stood up they began to tilt his chair. They placed two long poles through hoops on the chair then picked it up. They moved the chair toward the entry of the temple. The Captain and Mica and Celi backed away from Lord Enki. The old man walked toward the entry. The guards with the small tent followed him. Behind the tent slowly walked a tall ancient stick of a man. He was thin; he wore flowing robes. He wore a long red banner across his chest; the banner held the symbol for ⵅEnki. He spoke for Lord ⵅEnki. He was the lord's Vizier.

Mica remarked later that Lord Enki always walked. He did not require men to carry him everywhere as did Lord ⵅEnlil. When Celi asked about Lord ⵅEnlil, Mica said he was the Supreme High Lord of the Land. "His word is final," he added.

Lord Enki was almost to the entry when he stopped and looked up at the workers on the wall. Their scaffold was on the outside. What he saw was the upper bodies of seven men who were shaving stone to make it fit the wall. The wall was as high as six men, or 30 cubits tall. He called over his Captain and spoke into his ear.

The Captain of the Guards straightened his back and said loudly in the direction of the workers, "My Lord, the Lord Enki, on whose temple you labor, says, 'You honor me and you honor my temple with your work,' sayeth Lord Enki." [End Note 1]

Lord Enki turned and walked through the entry. The four guards with his small tent followed him. There was silence. The Lord never talked to the workers.

All eyes were on the procession when Celi heard a cry from near the wall and a loud noise like a large melon hitting stone. She turned and saw a workman, called Pana by his mates, lying on his back. His leg was bent at an angle under him; there was blood seeping from one ear.

Chapter 2

Celi walked quickly to the man. She heard the loud voices of two or three men above her on the wall. She began to kneel; Mica gave her a cloth for under her knees. She reached out and touched the man's arm. Pana did not react. His eyes were open but he stared at the top of the wall where two of his mates were in a loud argument. His eyebrows formed into a frown, as if he asked the question ...What happened?

Celi bent nearer to Pana and looked at his ear. A trickle of blood fell from his ear onto the white stone of the temple floor. She caught a whiff of his breath: stale beer. She bent down farther to look at the back of his head. There was a small puddle of blood. She watched the puddle. It did not grow.

The man groaned, softly. *'That is a good sign,'* she thought. *'If he feels pain, he is alive.'*

She used her hand to wave over his face. He did not move.

"Can you move your head?" she asked. Behind her Mica said "That may not be a good idea." Slightly behind her she saw the feet and sandals and bare legs of her grandfather. He wore his work tunic today, as on all days.

"Bring water," she commanded.

She heard more than saw Mica moving to the water jug where it was kept in the shade from the tall wall.

She looked at Pana. He seemed confused and troubled. He began to move his hand toward his head and she stopped him. His eyes suddenly opened wide. She saw his lips pull away when he ground his teeth together. A sound from deep inside his chest began to grow. He closed his lips. The sound grew until it burst through his lips in an enormous scream that drove four crows into flight from a palm tree outside.

Celi straightened up, away from the screaming man. She looked around and saw her grandfather bringing a jug of water. She looked up and saw men looking down from the top of the wall. *'Water, to clear his throat,'* she thought.

She reached up to take the jug from Mica. She looked at the jug. *It cannot hurt him.* A sudden revelation told her his head was hurt. The water would not hurt him. She put the jug to his lips and said, "Drink." His eyes turned and saw her, as if for the first time. He opened his mouth and she poured water. It gurgled and he managed to swallow before some water spilled out and ran down his cheek and onto the small puddle of blood near his ear.

"Go to the Lord's camp. Tell them we have an injured man."

She looked at Mica. He looked around and saw there was no one he could send. When he began to move toward the temple entry with its sixteen-foot-tall doors, Celi looked down at Pana and touched his face. She saw a reaction. He was looking directly into her eyes.

"You fell."

He did not react. A pain suddenly gripped him and he bit his lower lip. He bit the lip hard for what seemed, to Celi, like an eternity. Water squeezed out of his eyes. He made a fist and opened his fist and she grabbed his hand. He tightened his hand. *'Take his pain,'* she thought.

His fist squeezed her hand until it began to hurt. Then she felt his hand relax.

She waved her hand over his face. There was no reaction. *'He has gone to some other place,'* she surmised. She looked around. The woman with the broom had disappeared. She looked up. Three men were looking down. The two men who argued were out of sight. Long moments passed while he seemed to sleep peacefully.

Suddenly his eyes opened. His eyebrows went up. It was a startle reaction, as if he had suddenly realized where he was and what happened to him.

"He pushed me," said Pana

Celi did not react until, "I think you said..."

"He pushed me."

"What? ...oh, who?" she responded.

"Long ago ..." he paused, then added "...he was my..." and drifted off when his eyes rolled up into his head. After a time, he would grunt or groan and once he opened his eyes and tried to sit up. He managed to put both hands on the white marble of the floor and push himself up. Half-way to sitting up his eyes closed and he fell back. His head fell into the puddle of blood with a 'thunk.'

From behind Celi she heard the crunch of feet on the sand outside the temple. She heard footsteps on the stairway. She turned and saw Mica with a man dressed in the royal robes of Lord Enki's household staff. He wore a small cap that held his long flowing hair at the back of his head beneath a wreath of black cloth with golden emblems. His face looked grim.

He walked up to Celi with her grandfather trailing behind him. "You know me, I believe?" he directed at Celi.

He was the Lord's Vizier, a man with the power to write contracts and to settle minor disputes among the people.

Celi bowed slightly toward him while she knelt by Pana. She said nothing.

"How did this happen?"

"Lord Enki was leaving on his way back to his camp. We heard a man's cry and then Pana hit the floor."

"Do not seek to blame Lord Enki for this accident," said the Vizier while he brushed a few small mites of dust from the front of his long robe.

"I do not…" Celi began before the tall man with a face hardened by the sun looked directly at her and added, "I will report the accident." He turned to Mica and nodded as if to say, 'That settles the matter' as if he expected Mica to find an instant replacement on his work crew.

The Vizier waved a hand at a fly while he turned toward Mica and said, "Is there any dispute that I must settle?"

Mica stood with a blank face. This man was the Lord who directed the work on the temple. He held the power of life and death. In fact, just two weeks in the past he had a man executed who stole grapes and dates from Lord Enki's camp. And Mica and his crew spent one day repairing the hole in the camp wall. There were rumors the man actually stole the favors of one of Enki's wives while she was drunk.

The Vizier repeated his question. "Is there a dispute?"

Mica bowed to the Vizier and said in a quiet voice, "No, my Lord."

The Vizier turned to leave the temple. As he walked away Celi said in a loud voice, so the men on the wall could hear, "He said he was pushed."

The man turned with a frown on his face. He was not pleased. He looked at Celi for a long moment then said, "You wear the emblem of the royal family. You will talk to all of Mica's crew. Find out. They saw nothing. It was an accident. We will hold a tribunal this afternoon."

Celi looked down at Pana, where he struggled with the pain. His arms moved in a spasm. There was sweat on his forehead. "He is in pain," she said to the Vizier.

The Vizier nodded, as if to say 'he will not be at the tribunal.'

Celi began to stand. It was her intention to bow to the Vizier. As she stood Pana reached up and grabbed her arm. His eyes were open for a moment and he softly said, "My mate is . . ." and fell back. His eyes closed. Celi lifted his fingers off her arm and watched as his breathing slowed. There was one last gasp, then silence. She put her thumb against his neck.

After several moments she stood and bowed to the Vizier. Then she said, in a quiet voice with a certain amount of iron hard venom toward the man, "Our stone worker Pana will not attend. He is dead."

Chapter 3

Mica and Celi led a procession of six workers when they approached the walls of Lord Enki's camp, which resembled a walled compound. There were two guards at the entry gate. They challenged Mica to explain his business then led the group into the inner courtyard where Celi saw a beautiful tent stretched across half the courtyard. The tent's side panels were rolled up and tied to permit easy breezes to flow through. Three large rugs covered the ground immediately inside the tent. Toward the back a platform held a raised throne for the Lord.

Near the platform, to one side, sat a large white stone as high as a man's waist. Upon the stone sat a shallow stone bowl from which vapors and heat arose. The tendrils of smoke rose slowly in the light breeze until they passed through an opening at the top of the tent.

The guards stopped Mica and pointed at a spot in the middle of the rug. Mica moved to the spot. And knelt down. Celi followed his example and knelt behind him. The six workmen of Mica's crew formed a line behind Celi. They each wore their best tunic; their hands were washed and hair slicked back.

The Vizier appeared behind two guards who brought a small table. They set the table down. Two guards came behind with a small stool. A fifth guard brought a soft clay tablet and placed it upon the Vizier's table. The Vizier stood for a moment then announced in a strong voice, "The Lady Ninki approaches. Bow deeply."

The visitors to Enki's tent and the guards fell to their knees and brought their heads down upon their hands. The Vizier remained standing, as suited his status, and bowed from the waist. Celi heard the rustle of long gowns and looked up to see an aged and quite infirm woman being helped by two females. Her face held the scars called wrinkles by some but her face was peaceful and serene. She calmly watched as a smaller throne arrived directly behind her. Two men helped to sit. She sat and her attendants arranged her gown around her feet. One of the attendants placed a long cloth across her knees.

Without preamble the Lady said, "We begin."

A female attendant, dressed in a flowing white gown appeared from inside the residence of the Lord. She brought a small platter with grapes sitting on a bed of rice with leaves of eucalyptus under the rice. She proceeded to the stone altar, bowed toward Lady Ninki and pushed the offering onto the embers that burned inside the stone bowl. A white smoke began to rise.

To his audience the Vizier announced, "We honor the Lady Ninki, for she is the 'Lady of Green Plants'." [End Note 2]

To which Lady Ninki replied, "Yes, yes! Of course we do."

After her words were absorbed she added, "Seems like a waste of good grapes. This isn't a land flowing with grapes and dates."

To which the Vizier did not reply. After a silence stretched 'forever' Lady Ninki added, "We honor the Lord of Justice, Lord Enlil, who is Lord of the Land."

"Yes, of course we do," added the Vizier. He leaned over his clay tablet where he had been writing and said, "This day comes before the Lady Ninki the leader of the stone workers, Mica and his granddaughter Celi."

You have that wrong," said Lady Ninki, "as usual."

When the Vizier turned to look at her Lady Ninki added, "Her name is not Celi, it is *Celiste*, granddaughter of Ningal."

Celi turned her head. She was impressed by the old woman's pronunciation of her name, '*Say-Leest-Ay*.'

Celi bowed out of respect for the old lady while she tried to fathom how she came to be called 'Celiste.'

"It is your name, girl," said Ninki.

"Yes, as you wish," said Celi.

"I do not wish it. It is what it is," came the tart and sharp reply.

"Yes," remarked Celi.

"I am told you said 'He was pushed' and you challenged my Vizier's decision."

"She did not mean to challenge the Lord Vizier," said Mica quickly.

"The Vizier said it was an accident. I reported what the man said," added Celi.

There was a long period of silence. The Vizier walked back to Lady Ninki and spoke quietly into her ear.

Lady Ninki seemed to frown then said, "What he said was…?"

"I was pushed," Celi repeated. She looked around at the six men behind her and stopped on the man called Char. He stared back at her then dropped his head.

"Have you talked to the workers?" asked the Vizier.

"As you directed, oh mighty Vizier," remarked Celi.

Several mouths among the guards suddenly fell open. Lady Ninki began to smile before a raspy laugh issued forth.

"Yes, oh mighty Vizier," said Lady Ninki while laughing.

Unfazed the Vizier continued. "And what did you hear?" he asked.

"Of the twelve men on Mica's work crew, five were not on the scaffold yet. They were slow to arrive."

"And why is that?" said Lady Ninki.

"They were the last to leave after consuming an entire barrel of beer provided, I should add, by Lord Enki."

"It is what it is," said Lady Ninki. Her remark was made as if to allow that the past could not be changed. She knew her mate Lord Enki grew impatient with the slowness of the work on his temple.

"And these six men before us?" said the Vizier.

"Three of these men know nothing."

"And the remaining three?"

"One, Marlo, reports he heard the other two, Char and Seth arguing."

The Vizier stood silent. No questions came from behind him. He asked Marlo to step forward then said, "You say they argued?"

"My Lord Vizier, I do not know."

"Do not know?"

"I do not know why they argued."

"Did you hear any of their words?"

"Seth said 'You know his mate.' He said it twice. Then he said 'You were his friend'." The man Marlo said this while looking down at the ground.

At this Celi turned toward Marlo and asked if he knew that for a fact ...that they were friends.

"I think..." began Marlo before the Vizier stopped him with "Do not think. Tell us what you know."

"I do not know," said Marlo as he turned his face away from the Vizier's eyes.

Celi stepped toward the Vizier. "You mean to make him falter and doubt his words. How does that help us to find justice for Pana?"

"He is a Beag. It means 'short' for a reason. The Beag know their place. They look at the ground. That is all they know," added the Vizier.

At these words Lady Ninki seemed to revive and her head came up. She looked with a puzzled expression at Celi then asked, "Does Seth know?"

The sound of his name spoken by the divine goddess Ninki, mate of Lord Enki drove Seth to his knees. He felt like he wanted to bury his head and pray for forgiveness, both at the same time.

Celi stepped over to Seth and bent down toward his ear. "Tell us," she commanded.

"It is since then a long time," stammered the man.

"What is?" demanded the Vizier.

"A long time," repeated Seth.

"What do you say?" added the Vizier.

"They were friends since a long time in the past."

"Were they friends since Char came to Eridu?"

"I do not know," said Seth.

Celi patted his shoulder and urged him to stand up. While he pulled himself off the rug she said to the Vizier, "Pana said to me, and I tell you, he said 'Long ago,' and the words 'He was my...' but I do not know the meaning of his words. Did he refer to someone who was his friend? It may be the case."

"Get to the point," said Lady Ninki and she pointed at the workers. "Which one is Char?"

When no one replied Celi walked over and tapped Char on the shoulder. He looked at her then back at Lady Ninki. Char had a look that said, 'I am trapped.'

The Vizier was about to raise a question. Celi quickly said, "Did you push him?"

The Vizier stammered and stuttered and said, "You forget. I said it was an accident."

"I do not forget, oh mighty Vizier," she replied. To Char she posed the question this way, "Is it possible that something else happened?"

"I do not know," said Char.

"You do not know?" shouted the Vizier. To Seth he shouted, "Who was closest to Pana before he fell?"

Seth looked like he would prefer to vanish. He raised a hand and pointed at Char.

The Vizier slowly raised his arm and pointed at Char. "Did you push him?" he spat out in a loud voice. Nearby the crows flapped into the heavens, disturbed by the Vizier's tone of voice.

Char looked at the ground. He raised his head and said, "I do not know."

The Vizier lowered his arm. He looked at Char for a long time then back at Lady Ninki. When he turned back to Char he said, "Who told you to say that?"

There was shock on Char's face. His eyebrows went up. He saw Celi turn her head slightly, as if to say 'Be careful.'

"The Lady we work with. I trust her. She told me."

The Vizier turned ever so slowly toward Celi, as if he had a rabbit in sight and his bow pulled for a kill shot. Before he could say a word, Celi said with iron in her voice, "That is what he said when I asked him."

The Vizier was quick to seize his advantage. "In his words, then, he might have stumbled and it was an accident?"

Celi said nothing. She saw Lady Ninki was on her feet. The Vizier turned around to hear Lady Ninki say, "Enough. I give you my decision tomorrow."

The Vizier bowed at his waist and took two ceremonial steps backward. The rest of the participants did the same. Celi and Mica turned away and led their men out of the large compound that protected the two oldest of the lords.

Chapter 4

"Be brave," said Mica. They were standing outside their tent watching the workmen high on the scaffolding. The early sun painted the southern wall of the temple a light pink. Mica chewed on a long green stalk of water tuber, what some called Flash. Celi was busy pulling a brush through her hair.

"You were brave when Misha left us for the trip across the heavens."

"I was?"

"You were," he said smiling. In his mind he saw Celi's face when he told her. A tear formed in one eye. She made to go into Misha's sleeping room but he stopped her. She looked at Mica. He believed she began to realize that 'her Misha' would no longer cook and wash and comfort the two of them.

"Was I brave in Lord Enki's tent?"

"You were."

Mica watched her wind her hair into a bun. He helped her wrap her hair. She used an ancient blue wrap with gold bangles. The wrap looked festive. Mica knew she wanted to stand tall in front of Lady Ninki.

"Do not challenge the Vizier."

"He is full of himself. Full to brimming, like a vat of old beer."

"He is that," added Mica. A small crease at the corner of his mouth suggested he wanted to smile but restrained himself.

"Yes, my Mica," she said and patted his arm. "You watch over me."

Mica said nothing.

"You watch over all of us."

"I have to. Misha would not forgive me if something bad happened to you."

Celi looked directly at him. These was a sheen of water in both eyes. "She looks down upon us?"

"Yes."

"From someplace in the heavens?"

"She has gone to live with the Watchers, in the heavens."

Celi looked down at her feet. A tear drop fell straight down and splashed on her big toe. "I give water to the land."

"We all do," added Mica.

"And that Vizier, that old man with his three women."

"They are temple priestesses," said Mica.

"They occupy your house," said Celi. She had never recovered from the Vizier's decision to take Mica's house after Misha's death.

"He blamed me for her death," said Mica.

"You said she..." began Celi.

"...should have stayed off the platform that day."

"She brought you a meal."

"Yes. It was unusual. Not a big stone. But big enough."

"And she was quiet. Said not a word. For three days in her bed. Then you came out of her sleeping room and I knew."

"And two days later the Vizier came. Telling us Lord Enki had 'cast out' three of the temple women for not pleasing him." An eyebrow went up. "And would I shelter the three women until we found spouses for them?"

"As if it was our duty?" said Celi.

"And they arrived with trunks. And padded chairs. And three slave women. A whole house of women," he laughed.

"I much prefer this old tent. It is quiet."

She smiled at her grandfather. When she turned toward the village she saw one of the 'temple women' arguing with a man who was trying to give her a sheep. "Huh," she snorted, "He does not know she cannot touch a living being. She is a priestess."

Mica turned to look in the same direction. He smiled and said, "Be with charity. She knows only her own rules."

"Yes, she knows how to work on her back," laughed Celi.

"And does not know the butcher's blade," added Mica with a laugh.

Chapter 5

In mid-morning Celi received a message. The young man wore a bright red tunic, a royal color for the House of Enki. He found Celi working beside Mica near the Temple. The message he delivered required her to bring Char and Seth and Mica to Lady Ninki's fore-court at the camp at mid-afternoon. She could not know that today her life would introduce many fascinating challenges.

Celi took the three men to the river to wash. She wore a white robe that protected her modesty. The river was shallow close to shore but deeper and running fast farther out. She waded in and turned her back to the men.

Mica told Seth and Char to wash up. They dropped their tunics and sandals on the shore and waded in with a washing cloth. Mica saw their nakedness and swore a small curse; he told them to turn their backs to Celi. Mica stood there and shook his head in disbelief. "Rotten morons!" he cursed.

"Is that the best you can do?" laughed Celi. She looked over her shoulder at Mica and winked. He said nothing.

When Celi and the three men stepped onto the rug under the tent, they found a young man sitting cross-legged off to the side. He had a platter in front of him that held grapes, dates, baked fish and broiled mutton. He paused with a piece of melon to look at Celi and began to smile. She had known him forever. He ran with the group of boys that teased her. He was Deem, the student pilot. He wore the white tunic of a student; his legs and arms and face were the color of bronze. His face had the proud bearing of a member of Lord Enki's family.

A scene flashed through her mind. Deem had a girl on each arm. They were about to enter the temple in Ur when a priest objected.

Celi began to smile at Deem then thought, *'Wait, he is dangerous.'* Celi did not know why she grabbed that thought in passing. She ignored him.

A servant girl in a white tunic with the red band at the hem appeared. She brought a platter with grapes, dates, fish, mutton and large chunks of melon. She also brought a jug containing beer and placed it on the rug between the men. *'What?'* Celi thought. *'They expect me to drink out of the same jug as these men?'* At that moment she felt she was being foolish but remembered her grandmother Misha's oft-repeated parable, 'Those who sleep with the Beag will become a Beag.' [End Note 3]

Celi looked at Seth and Char after they sat on the rug. Their brow ridges were distinct; there was no doubting they were descended from the men and women who worked in the mines. They were shorter, husky with strong arms and backs. They were brought north when Lord Enki asked for strong workers to rebuild his temple.

"That man," said Deem, "who thinks he runs the world, said wait."

Mica without missing a beat spit out "To which of us do you speak?"

"The young lady."

"And what gives you the right to address my granddaughter?"

"Her straight back."

"Her what?"

"She carries herself as if she owns the world, much as does that Vizier."

Mica said nothing. He tried to glance at Celi to see if she was offended. Her face was a blank. She sat down; she said nothing.

"Well, she does," said Deem. He finished his melon and picked up a towel to dry his fingers. He raised a piece of mutton and sniffed it. Then he began to tear into it.

Celi leaned over toward her grandfather and softly said, "Perhaps this is not the place to pick a fight with a stranger."

"I know him," remarked Mica. "And so do the young ladies of Eridu."

"And so do I," she added and thought, *Tell Mica about the temple guards.*

She reached out and patted Mica's arm saying, "Peace." Celi nodded toward the back of the tent where the Lord's Vizier had appeared. He cleared his throat to announce his presence. When he had their attention he said, "Bow low. The Lady Ninki comes."

Those present went up on their knees and bent forward into the posture of respect. The Vizier walked slowly from the back then stepped onto the platform. He was trailed by a young man, a scribe. The guards brought his small table and stool. The scribe carefully placed his clay tablet and prepared to record the day's events. Behind them came Lady Ninki with two attendants and two guards with her throne. When she was seated she looked around the small gathering and said, "Arise to receive my decision."

To Deem she said, "Come forward."

The young man walked up to the edge of the platform and knelt on the edge. He bowed his head. Lady Ninki looked at him for a long moment before she declared, "Raise your head. Lord Enki declares that you are a pilot with the privileges that come with your position. You are assigned Second Position to Captain Shar on the vehicle we call *Dara.* You will join the *Dara* for more training."

Deem bowed his head and said, "Thank my Lord Enki. I will serve as you wish."

Lady Ninki smiled. "That is what I wish. Further, you are known to be full of yourself. Learn to accept advice from Captain Shar. Be humble. Be honest."

All he could do was nod. Celi saw his face turn red with her rebuke.

"Now leave."

Deem stood up, backed away from the platform then turned to leave the tent. As he walked by Celi she saw him raise his hands to his face. *'Face is hot,'* she noted.

Lady Ninki wasted no time. She called Seth forward and asked him if he had changed his statement. 'No,' he replied. He did not know if Char had a reason to push Pana from the top of the wall. Then she surprised the gathering by asking the scribe to repeat the statement made by Pana's mate that morning.

The scribe squinted at his tablet. "Statement by the mate of Pana. We were friends long past, twenty years ago. We were lovers. I chose Pana to be my mate. Char was upset but he loved Pana like a brother. No, he did not push Pana. It had to be an accident."

The Vizier stood taller above his clay tablet and smiled. "As I said."

"Your decision is only a guess," said Lady Ninki from behind him.

His smile slowly wilted. He busied himself flicking dust off his royal robe.

She told Char to come forward and said, "Did you push him?"

"Lady," he began. "I wish I know how to tell you. I will take care of Pana's mate. I will be her mate tomorrow and all the days ahead."

"Did you push him?" she repeated.

"There was a stone. My foot came down on the edge. My foot began to make me fall. I reached out. Pana was there. My hand hit him in back."

There was silence while Lady Ninki waited to see what else Char would say. He was silent. She looked at Celi and said,

"Is this man truthful?"

"He knows only to tell what he knows."

Celi thought about that comment for a moment then added, "Mica says to report Char is a good worker, a little slow to understand, but he does as he is told."

Lady Ninki raised a hand and closed her fist. It was a symbol that she required all present to listen to her decision. The scribe glanced around and saw her raised arm and said, "All present. Hear the decision of Lady Ninki."

"Let your tablet record my words. Char is sentenced to three years to serve as a guard at Arad, a small village west of the White Sea. During these three years you will not once touch a woman. If you do the first penalty shall be the loss of one hand. On the second occasion you will have your manly parts removed so that no one will ever have to wonder if you desired a certain woman who you just declared you would be a mate to. This is my decision. You contributed by your negligence to the death of Pana."

"Seth and his mate will also serve as guards. The three of you and Celiste will spend the next ten days training with our hunting rifles. You will learn to hit a radish at fifty paces."

Mica was about to object when Lady Ninki added, "I will talk to you and Celiste privately." And she waved at the guards and attendants and the scribe and told them to leave her with Mica and Celiste.

Chapter 6

The very moment they were alone with Lady Ninki she coughed then laughed in a high pitched voice. “For an old man you seem to be wise?” she chattered.

Mica bowed down. He was confused.

“Are you wise?” asked Ninki.

Mica bowed again.

“Are you bowing to my decision? Or are you a mite insubordinate?”

“I have been honored to build Lord Enki’s temple.”

“But?” she asked.

“Why do you take my granddaughter away?”

There was silence. Ninki sat up straighter in her chair, if that was possible. Celi took two steps back, momentarily afraid of the older woman’s wrath.

Ninki raised a hand as if to say ‘Peace.’ “It is possible that this old man pleases me when he asks a question with merit.”

“Before you hurt your back, stand up,” she directed at Mica.

The old man straightened up with a low groan.

“Many and a few years building temples is my guess,” said Ninki.

Mica nodded.

"Hear me now." She walked to the scribe's table and picked up a small roll of papyrus on which a small seal had been attached. She walked to the front of the platform and held it out to Celi.

Celi took the scroll and unrolled it and began to slowly read the contents.

"Listen to me now, Celiste."

Celi raised her eyes to the ancient face of her mistress.

"Celiste, granddaughter of Ningal, you are 6th generation from Enoch. Your mother was Ishtar, the mother of Inanna, who serves the Temple of Isis. I am not permitted to tell the name of your father. You are Rank 25 and would sit on the Council of 12 should Ningal die. Lord Enki and I have a special task for you."

She noticed that Celi's mouth had opened. *'I did not expect...'* thought Celi.

"For the next 10 days, you and Char and Seth will practice with our rifles. We can only send two rifles to Arad. You will take command and rebuild the village. The women there lost their men who were taken to join the Army of Abram. Char and Seth and Seth's mate will serve as guards."

"Why are they guards?" asked Mica.

"Twenty-four females with no men. Why would you have guards?"

Mica thought for a moment. "Ah, I see," he said. He felt an old lump on his arm and wondered. "Are there no temple women?"

"A small temple, no temple women," said Lady Ninki. Celi looked down at the rug on which she stood. Her face masked her turmoil. *Must I leave my Mica?*

"Your face shows your distress?" asked Ninki.

"Yes, I..." began Celi but thought better of it. "I worry ...my grandfather Mica."

"Has served my Lord and Master, Enki, with satisfaction."

"But my Mica..." she began.

"Will finish the temple for Lord Enki."

"Yes," said Ninki. *He will build a landing floor in Arad,* thought the Lady. *He must finish first Lord Enki's temple. My master is impatient.*

"There is one man, his mate and his daughter ...caretakers."

"And a royal princess from Salem."

"But Salem, I have heard, is a large city?" said Celi.

"It is. Very large."

"Does not this princess resent being in Arad?"

Ninki smiled and clapped. "I told Lord Enki you were smart. Now you see it."

"So you want me to direct the village."

"Yes."

"And the women? They are...?"

"Beag. Good strong women. They came north from the mines." [End Note 4]

"And the fields?"

"Were planted before the men were taken."

"So there is no one in Arad who is of royal birth?"

"Only the princess. And she desires to leave."

Celi looked at Mica and said, "It is Lady Ninki's wish that I take control over this village. I shall want one, ...no two ...friends who are Aryan, like me."

"Lady Ninki, thank you for the honor." Celi was quiet for a long moment. "May I make one request?"

"Yes."

"My good friend Gran and her friend Harn, if he chooses to join us."

"That is my wish," said Ninki quietly.

Ninki turned and watched the scribe. He was carefully recording the wish of his mistress into the wet clay of his tablet. His stylus was a reed with a point the allowed him to record words into the clay. He finished and sat up straight.

"It is recorded, as my Lady wished.

Chapter 7

Celi and Gran met when they were six years old. Gran's parents directed the village market; they had grown in Eridu and pledged and brought forth six children, two boys and four girls. Gran was their youngest; she kept the family in stitches. She was the one child who always asked 'why?' and she was the first to defend her siblings. When her brothers found mates her father rejoiced. Quietly he worried about the cost of pledging four young daughters.

Gran's jaw dropped when she heard what Celi had requested.

"You said what?" said her friend Gran in a slightly louder voice.

"That I want you with me."

"No."

"Yes, I did say that."

"What I meant was No with a drum roll."

"It would please Lady Ninki that you and Harn go with me."

"And Harn? Did you think to ask him?"

"No."

"Celi, my friend Celi, tell me why you asked for Harn."

"It is no secret in Eridu. That is why," added Celi with a small laugh.

"No secret. Even your parents know you have seen Harn."

"No?"

"Yes," said Celi. "The sun was rising. Two of our stone workers saw you climbing a ladder to the roof over your parent's house."

"But we cannot go. We are not..."

"A ceremony can be held. Your parents will receive a modest dowry."

"On short notice?"

"Your father will save what for him is a fortune. A brief ceremony."

"The entire village will think that I must have dishonored my family," said Gran while she glanced around. They were standing at the base of the stairway to the temple. Gran tugged at her short robe, as if someone in Eridu might object to her manner of dress.

Celi reached up and tucked a strand of Gran's hair back under her head wrap. She put her hand on Gran's shoulder and squeezed it. Gran had a pleasant face, even what some would call beautiful. Her black hair and light hazel eyes were complimented by her ready smile. Celi could easily see how Harn had fallen for her.

"Will it matter what they think?" Celi asked but Gran said, "Who?"

"People in this ancient dump heap with its half buried houses and broken port."

"If I had a reason..." said Gran.

Celi looked at her. She laughed. Gran looked at Celi and began to smile.

"You are a baker," said Celi.

"We need your skills and Harn likes what you make in your oven."

"Yes, ...I know. He likes what I do with chopped apples and a dough mixture with cinnamon and, well ..."

"Think of it as an adventure," added Celi before she said, "And we may get to see that dashing young pilot Deem. He was promoted."

"Dashing?" said Gran.

"My word," answered her friend.

"Dashing is correct. He dashes after the un-mated ladies. He should be mated by now. What age has he reached?"

"He celebrated his twelfth year when I celebrated my sixth birthday, shortly after coming here from Nippur."

"That makes him twice twelve," said Gran.

Gran wrinkled up her nose. "Bleah! He is an old man."

Chapter 8

"He had no choice?" said Celi while she walked up the slope to Enki's temple. She wore her long red robe over a white tunic. Her hair was bound in a long cloth with red and white stripes. On her right shoulder she wore the silver circle with seven green gems, her badge of rank. As she approached the lower stairs to the temple the guard must have realized she held rank. He said something to the other guard and they both stood taller.

Next to her Gran stopped. She reached out to stop Celi and said, "No choice?"

"Deem had no choice. The Lord Abram caught him."

"Doing what"

"Leaving the temple in Ur."

"But doing what"

"He was leaving with two of the temple women."

Celi laughed. She and Gran walked up the steps to the second platform, then crossed the short 'porch' and started up the second stairs.

Gran slowly asked, "Is that the Abram...?"

"Who fought in the War of the Kings?" said Celi. "Yes."

"My uncle was in his troop. They mounted onto camels and attacked the army of the Hittite kings?"

"And drove the Hittite army back to Damascus." Celi smiled. The history of the most recent war with the Hittites was well known. [End Note 5]

"So Lord Abram caught him?"

"Judged him on the spot." Celi smiled. She could still hear Mica telling the story about the brash young Deem on the street in Ur. "Ur was Abram's town."

"Lord Abram had five of his officers with him. One drew a sword and waved it at Deem." In her mind Celi saw the scene of Deem with two women surrounded by tall men with swords.

"Abram said, my Mica reports, 'You women will go with my officers who will punish you for leaving the sacred precincts of the temple,' as Mica says it.

Gran looked sideways at Celi with a frown. Her eyebrows inched together. She pulled her short working robe together and looked back at the guards. They were watching the two women.

"Does that mean?"

"Mica was protecting me. But I know what he meant."

"So the two women were made to 'pay tribute' for their mistake?"

"Probably one day, two at the most, in the tents of the officers."

Gran smiled at the thought. "And Deem?"

"A longer sentence for violating the sacred temple by trying to remove two of its temple women," said Celi. "That was three years ago."

"And?"

"His choice was join Enlil's Army in the Sinai or join the Din.Gir."

"Din.Gir?"

"I had to ask Mica. He says 'Righteous Ones of the Blazing Rockets,' he told me."

"A pilot?"

"And ordered to take the training. And touch not another woman until he is promoted to the level of Din.Gir, or pilot."

"Palms and Dates," remarked Gran.

"Yes, that young man. In an empty desert he will seek palms and dates."

Gran smiled. She glanced at Celi. Her face seemed sad.

"Be not sad for him, my friend."

Celi looked up. She saw Harn standing with Mica near the great door of the temple. She walked toward them. A nearby guard said something and the three men turned toward Celi and Gran. Celi saw the beginning of an enormous smile on Harn's face.

"Not sad for Deem. And as for Harn …he will get what he desires."

Gran smiled. Mica looked at Celi and knew his world was about to change.

Chapter 9

Mica and Celi stood in the grove of old palms near the temple. He could see his workmen on the top of the scaffolding. They were preparing to mount crossbeams that would serve as the base for the roof. They worked to build a tripod to lift the beams from the floor inside the temple. He smiled. The long beams were the trunks of 'very straight' cedar trees brought from a land near the western sea.

"Someday, my plan is to clean out the dead trees and replant younger palms to form a small clearing in the middle of this grove. It would be a place to think about the future and to enjoy the day."

"I will remember," said Celi.

She brought him to the 'stumps' as they called it. Someone in an ancient time had cut three palms and used three sections to make a bench. The old wood placed across the stumps was cracked, warped and about to fall off the stumps.

Celi led him toward the 'stumps' and he sat with a smile.

"The pain is less," he said.

She knew his back began to hurt, usually after mid-day. Sitting relieved some of the pain. When she looked in his eyes she knew he worried about her leaving.

Celi placed her hand under his arm and leaned to put her head on his shoulder. She thought for a moment, *'I should be sad,'* but realized *'I am excited.'* She did not know what the future held but she knew her 'Mica' was safe here in Eridu.

"I feel pain," she said quietly.

"I also. You are leaving."

"After Gran and Harn are pledged."

"You will be a far distance from here."

"Perhaps," she began. Her hope that the 'high lord' would send 'her Mica' to Arad after Enki's temple was built might be a very small possibility. "You will finish the temple."

"My role in life is to serve the Lord ӾEnki," he ritually intoned.

"Your desire to serve speaks much," she added.

"It was the agreement your Misha made when you came to us. She asked for me and I agreed." He smiled. There were images of 'his' Misha in a flowing white gown with yellow and white water lilies draped across her shoulders. There were images of their first days after they pledged. There were happy memories of the little girl who entered their lives and gave it purpose.

"We were happy. We had you, my Celi. We hoped but never received a baby. Misha was saddened by this."

"Did she say…?"

"No. I could see it in her eyes."

"I will always remember. And think of you here in this grove.

"I am sad," he said without thinking. "I have always liked Gran. Such a good friend."

"Gran and I and Harn. We will have three guards with two rifles."

"To protect the Beag women at Arad?"

"To protect all of us."

"Be careful. I hear there are deserters from the Army of Enlil."

"And other men of careless character, who like to attack women," she added while an image of Misha flared through her mind.

"Officer, from the barge," said Mica.

When she said nothing he added, "All the men were at the port, unloading long beams and the white stone for the temple floor."

He felt her hands come together on his arm. He tried to look down but could not see her face. "He seemed so nice. He came to the door looking for food," she told me later that day. Mica saw a cut on her neck, bruises on her arms.

"He ate some stew and bread then told me 'Come here.' When I resisted he said, 'I am Aryas. You serve me'."

"Misha was badly cut. She showed me how he held a knife at her throat while he 'punished her' for her insolence, not once but twice."

He felt her shoulders fall and wished he had not told her. "Always remember. The Aryas can be arrogant. I think that is the word."

"I will remember." She was silent while she tried to absorb Mica's words. "Did he think our Misha was Beag?"

"She was out in the sun working in the fields. Her hair was much lighter; her skin was darker, the darkest she had ever been, except around her hips."

"He might have known she was Aryas?"

"And did not care." He raised his arm and swung it around her shoulders. They sat in silence while the sun marched down the western sky. In his mind Mica saw his beloved, pale against an old blanket. "Her voice grew weak. At the last she said, 'Take care of Celi'." He paused. "I have honored my promise."

"You have, my brave Mica" She leaned back into him and placed her head against his chest. "Always. You have been my father."

She felt a sob coming up and stifled it. Her head shook while she cried. He brought his hand up and held her head.

"When I can no longer work I will come to Arad."

"I will ask for a stone worker for Arad."

"Lord Enki's Vizier will not agree."

"I will ask," she said with a hopeful, cherished smile.

Chapter 10

Gran and Harn stood and faced each other. Her robe of white cotton fell to her feet; a string of orange and yellow flowers stretched from shoulder to shoulder. Her black hair held a clutch of white lilies. Harn looked somewhat official dressed in the 'uniform' of white tunic with red piping on the sleeves, over black trousers. He wore a cotton cap with a red band. They stood in the shade from a group of leafy trees in a park. The park was on high ground, a survivor from the last flood.

She smiled and reached up to touch his cap. His eyes displayed a twinkle; she thought he looked scared.

"The cap is to tell those who do not know that I am an official."

"You mean," she began, "I cannot believe it? I have to take orders from you?"

"Well..." he stuttered.

She laughed. She brought her hand down and caressed his face.

They stood on a stretch of grass under leafy date palms. Their friends stood around them. Gran's parents held a place of honor under a tent decorated with garlands of flowers. They sat on chairs on a platform where they would receive guests after the ritual of mutual pledges was finished.

"We are both assistants to our Lady Celi. She is the royal blood here."

"Yes, I know," said Gran.

"As far as taking orders..."

"Harn ...will you judge not my words harshly?"

"Why?"

"I wanted you to smile. Even a little. You look strange."

"This is more than I expected," he said looking around. There was a rug under their feet. An altar stood nearby to receive offerings to Inanna, Goddess of Love. Their friends looked expectant. A scribe would record their wedding on an official tablet and the tablet would be hardened in a kiln.

"Hard to believe. So much food." He glanced at the long tables under a long tent where small stools stood waiting.

"You men," she laughed. "There is one thing *only* on your mind."

"You mean my friends. They like to eat. I paid for two barrels of beer."

"Yes. A bit extravagant," she chuckled. "But I forgive you."

She saw his left hand begin to twitch; she took his hand in hers. She looked up at her nervous fellow and said, "Now."

From back inside the crowd behind her someone said, "Bout time. No more stalling."

Harn's head snapped up. He looked in the direction of the voice. "Pay him no mind," said Gran.

"My cousin Flare," said Harn. "Typical. Fourth cousin. A wine maker."

Someone nearby said "Your pledge," to push Harn to his task.

There was a pause. The small crowd around the two friends became quiet.

"I pledge," began Harn. "To spend all my days in devotion of this woman, to stand at her side against foul weather, to love and cherish her children..."

Someone in the crowd said, "Does she have children?"

There was a loud sound of a thwack and someone groaned.

"And to be faithful to my mate Gran."

Someone among four men who held jugs of beer said, "Bout time."

Several other men laughed. It was known that Gran had been seen leaving Harn's small house very early in the morning for the last two months.

"I pledge," began Gran, "to allow you to spend your days in devotion to me," she snickered, "But also to stand by your side and to love *your* children."

Harn looked at her.

Gran reached up to caress his face again. "You said devotion *of* this woman. Your words were to be *devotion to* but I believe we will be partners."

She took both of his large hands in hers and said, "I accept your pledge."

"And I accept your pledge," he added.

And thus the ceremony was ended.

"And now the food," said Harn to his relief.

"And here comes the *Dara,*" said Celi.

From the north they heard the distant rumble of engines when they cracked and popped as the pilot backed off his throttles. The park stood next to a long broad avenue that served as a road and a landing place for flying vehicles. Those who had to leave on the *Dara* knew they had a few minutes while the pilots surveyed the long avenue to drive off any stragglers. Someone blew a horn to announce evacuation of King's Road. End Note 6

Eridu is an ancient city. It sits on the edge of an enormous delta where the Euphrates River spreads over low lands and small islands. It has been flooded many times from the over-flow of the river. In the more distant past a great flood swamped the city for two years. The south-west quadrant holds the remains of small houses half-buried in mud and sand and gravel. The town is a sacred site, sacred to those who believe ⚹Enki is a divine god. They write his name with a star symbol to indicate his divinity.

In the center of the city stands the temple mount. On this mound of rubble and debris sits the temple where Mica's crew and three other crews labor each day to help the temple 'rise from the ashes' on her older foundations. North of the temple the city spreads out on both sides of a broad, straight avenue called King's Road that runs to the northwest. This is the road used by merchants to bring goods to the sacred cities of the Aryan lords: Ur, Lagash and Nippur.

New houses are built; the bath houses (for men only) have been rebuilt. There is a center where cut wood is dried for the kilns and baking ovens. A large compound surrounds the kilns where river clay becomes fire-hardened bricks. An even larger compound inside high walls has tall chimneys of brick where hot fires once melted gold ore and produced ingots.

Along the western edge of King's Road is the daily market place where slaves are allowed to purchase vegetables and meat for their owners. The park where the ceremony took place stands on the eastern flank of the avenue. When the *Dara* passed overhead, all activity ceased. People craned their necks to see her bulbous, round shape.

Dara went over the city to the east then turned up river to the north. She came to the west in a large circle that allowed her to line up with King's Road. She seemed to float in an action that stopped her descent before she came straight down on the road.

Celi saw her body was shaped like a blunt cone; the top of *Dara* was curved across the top of the round body. She had short wings that were folded into the body when she landed. Her main engines shut down when she was twenty cubits above the road. A set of four smaller engines slowed her descent until her legs settled on the road. Dust blew in every direction; dust swirled around the small tents in the market. Two men stood near the celebration tent and held it in place while the tent covers snapped from the sharp wind. She saw small square windows along the side of the shuttle. Celi saw one metal pole antenna and knew a second was on the other side.

The *Dara* came down while three sets of struts projected from within her body. The back struts touched the King's Road and the entire vehicle seemed to bounce upward then settle back onto the road. The third strut came to rest; *Dara* was down. She threw up a large cloud of dust. Then she sat quietly. An engine popped as it cooled.

A ramp lowered from between the engines. Two guards dressed in the red uniforms of the royal house exited from *Dara*. They went to opposite sides of the flying vehicle where they took up stations to protect *Dara* with their hand weapons.

Behind them came two officers in black uniforms. They wore black boots into which they tucked their trouser legs. They wore black coats of thick material on which was mounted the 'seven starred' emblem of the royal family. [End Note 7] The lead officer had a face of old granite under his gray hair. The second officer, with an enormous smile on his charming face was Deem.

"Who is that?" asked Gran.

"Which one?" laughed Celi.

"The young one?"

"That is Deem. He has a very high opinion of himself, as you will see," remarked Celi. Then she described the older pilot Shar, a veteran of many years.

"You just pledged yourself," stated Celi in a sarcastic tone.

"True. But I have friends," said Gran. "Three of them are not pledged."

Celi and Gran and Harn and their friends watched the two officers as they walked to the tent and congratulated Gran's parents. Then they turned toward the tables of food and began to load melon and grapes onto a platter, to which they added roasted mutton and baked fish.

"Just like men," noted Celi.

Harn raised an eyebrow as if to say, "Is that true?"

Gran said, "Wait. Perhaps ...they left their port at sunrise this morning. They had no morning meal. The sun is almost at mid-day. Can you blame them?"

"Gran, you are always ready to defend."

"That is my role. I will challenge you if I believe you are wrong."

Harn looked at the two women and raised a hand to scratch his eyebrows. Behind his hand he stifled a laugh. Gran saw his reaction and slapped his arm. He raised his eyebrows this time in a look that said, "What did I do?"

Chapter 11

Gran and Harn moved to the long table of food. Celi saw three of Harn's friends trying to give him small jugs of wine or beer. She laughed. She could see his friends were happy for him. Gran turned to place a small piece of melon in his mouth. Harn laughed and showed her a jug he grabbed from one of his friends. Then he opened his mouth to receive the melon.

Celi watched as Gran nodded. *'Gran and Harn ...can she control him?'*

As soon as the couple had their 'mating' platter filled with melon and grapes and fish, their friends surrounded the long table. Their friends for the most part wore white 'work-day' trousers under their best tunics. Their tunics and jackets were a profusion of yellows with light green trim or bright green with dark blue trim. The ladies wore their hair in buns held by fancy bands of cloth, some with silver or gold medallions.

Celi noticed her new guards were over by the large barrel of beer drinking from small bowls. From somewhere they had found black trousers to wear under their white tunics and very old, faded red caps. Their clothing packs and the two rifles were hidden. As she walked over toward Char and Seth she noticed the smile on Char's face and thought, *'yes, good beer.'* Char gave his bowl to Seth and turning toward Celi made an elaborate deep bow.

"Did you notice there are only a few Beag at this gathering?"

"No, Lady."

"That is Lady Celiste to you," she said with a grim face.

"Yes, Lady." Char's lips seemed to curl in a sneer.

"Did you not hear me?"

"Yes, Lady Celiste," said Seth. He moved to the table near the barrel and placed his bowls on the table.

"And who invited you to drink, what is it?"

"It is beer, Lady Celiste.

"Thank you, Seth. I asked 'Who invited you?' just now."

"No one, my Lady."

"Then go and get your things and my rifles and take them to the ramp at the back of *Dara*."

"Yes, my lady," added Char. He did not smile.

"And then move my small chest from the platform over to the ramp."

Neither man said a word. They had turned toward the small clump of trees where Seth's mate Dana had been guarding the rifles and their clothes.

She watched them for a moment thinking *'that man Char will cause trouble,'* and then remembered the proverb, 'There are smart dogs who know not to trust the Beag.'

In the corner of her eye she saw Gran and Harn near the pilot Deem. They held empty platters. Celi began to walk toward them when she heard Gran say, "Half-fill the platter and take it across King's Road. A family over there would like to eat as we are eating today."

Deem looked at her then at his platter and said, "I can fill it."

"Yes, I know you can," answered Gran. It was an ages old mantra.

"But I cannot eat it," said Deem.

"Tell it to those across the road."

Celi had heard the same mantra at mating ceremonies often repeated. They were intended to teach humility among those who have much.

Deem was reluctant. "Are there no women servants here?"

"You mean women Beag, I believe?" Celi answered.

"Yes," he said scanning the crowd.

"No Beag. There is Dana over there in the trees," commented Celi.

"But?"

"Dana has a role to play. She is a guard."

"She could…"

"No, she has two rifles to protect."

'This man is impossible,' thought Celi. It seemed obvious that he did not want to walk across King's Road to deliver food to people who were far below his station. Deem stood in front of Celi holding his loaded platter.

Harn came over, probably drawn by the look of consternation on Celi's face. She looked at Harn and nodded her head toward Deem. "It would please me if you would perform the platter ceremony," she smiled at Harn.

Harn glanced back at Gran and saw she was talking to their guests. Harn took the platter from Deem and walked toward the market center.

"As you wish, my Lady."

Deem raised an eyebrow. "My lady?"

"You mean why the 'my Lady?' …in his response?"

"It was improper."

"Harn is a distant cousin. He is a friend. He respects me. I respect him."

"And me? What of me?"

"I do not know you, Deem. I know of you."

At these words Deem stood a little taller.

"I know only of your reputation."

"I am Pilot Second to Captain Shar of the *Dara,* my Lady."

"And a slow learner." She said these words without anger. Celi knew there were men who think only of themselves and seldom give a thought about others.

"My Lady Celi," said Deem slowly with a slight bow. He sought to redeem himself to this royal princess who was not afraid to dress him down. "Where is your mate?" he added.

"Your questions betray your ignorance," she snapped at him.

Deem froze. He saw Captain Shar waving a finger to mean 'Get on with it.'

Deem shook his head in exasperation and was about to say something in response but stood taller and announced. "Those going to Arad, meet me here."

He saw Gran coming toward him in her flowing robe and shook his head. "Lady, excuse my manner. It will be cold in *Dara.*"

"I need trousers?"

"And one heavy wrap," noted Deem. Looking up from her shapely figure Deem saw Seth, Dana and Char approaching.

"You three?" he said. He noticed Char looking around.

"Yes, us. We have two rifles."

"Place them on the floor behind the Captain. Then go back to Cargo."

As he turned away Char said, "*Cargo?*"

"That is what you are. Cargo. Sit with your back to the wall. Hold your clothes on your lap. Do not talk to anyone. Protect the Lady's chest and bedding and coats."

They turned to go. Celi waited a long moment before she said, "You are harsh, young Pilot Deem."

"Not harsh, *my Lady Celi*." He paused. She thought *'Yes, he said it.'*

"But realistic. If we have trouble and I need to lighten my *Dara*, they are where I can throw them out of the cargo door."

"Throw who?" said Harn as he returned from the market.

"Not who, but what," remarked Deem. "They are cargo."

Harn stopped in his tracks. "Cargo?" He seemed puzzled until he realized Deem referred to Seth, Char and Dana.

"I hope you will discover, Pilot Deem, that some of us look at the Beag members of our villages as fellow workers," said Harn forcefully.

"Well said my 'Assistant' Harn," stated Celi in a firm voice.

Chapter 12

They were just below the clouds when the Captain announced "Everyone in seats." The launch of *Dara* had been uneventful. Celi and her friends felt the pull back into their seats when the *Dara* began to climb and accelerate. She heard a whimper from Dana in the back, but the 'cargo' was quiet and subdued by the power of *Dara.*

Several minutes into the flight Deem opened the door to the Captain's deck and asked Lady Celiste to talk to Captain Shar. She began to move up the passage but encountered the two rifles lying on the deck. She moved to her left but realized she would have to squeeze past 'Pilot Second' Deem to get to the Captain.

Deem smiled at her and offered her his hand. She ignored him and tried to squeeze by. She was looking into his eyes and wondering where his hands were when *Dara* suddenly jumped. She found herself up against Deem and felt his hands on her waist. He held her briefly until she put a hand on his arm and pushed him aside.

"You may use 'My lady' but do not assume we are friends," she said in a rush of embarrassment and anger at having touched him.

An eyebrow rose on Deem's face and he smiled.

Celi took two steps up the passage then turned back to Deem and added, "And do not smile at me."

She took two more steps up to the Captain's chair and heard him say, "What was that? You said, 'Do not smile' I believe."

"You must instruct your brash young pilot not to touch a woman, especially not a woman with royal blood."

Captain Shar was silent for a long moment while he chose a response. Then he said, "There is something you must know."

Celi said, "Yes?"

"We flew across Arad this morning. The fields look good. The crops are coming up. But there are no horses, no wagons at Arad."

"That will be a problem."

"Yes it will. We saw one woman at the river and a man appeared to be fishing."

"Those must be the two I was told about," she said.

"That would be my guess."

"And the women?"

"In the fields, scattered about."

"Captain," she said quickly. "What were your orders for this trip?"

He was silent. He reached out and pulled the throttles back minutely. The *Dara* was flying level with her wings extended and the clouds were gone. Celi looked out the forward windows and saw brown and green patches underneath them. Ahead she saw mountains.

"I am to offer you all assistance."

Captain Shar did not add that he was told she was going to a primitive village which needed to be rebuilt; the men were gone; and Lady Celiste may need help.

"Can you change course?"

"To where?"

"Salem."

Captain Shar thought for a moment until he said, "Yes, we will fly up the main valley of these mountains until we turn west toward Salem."

Then he added, "May I ask why?"

"To purchase vegetables and some meat, for Arad, maybe some beer."

"And?" he said thinking she missed the obvious.

"Two wagons and four horses and fishing nets."

"Ah," he responded quietly. "I see."

He did not tell her that such things were in short supply. Many wagons and horses went south with the men recruited for Enlil's Army down in Tilmun. Almost all the iron and bronze and copper in the entire region had been forged into swords or lance heads for the men who were training.

Shar turned around and said to Deem who was standing in the passage, "Return to your station. We will turn."

"To where?" said Deem as he slid past Celi and lowered himself into his seat. He took hold of the steering bars and said, "Yes, Captain?"

"Thirty-five degrees to the northeast. We go to Salem." [End Note 8]

To Celi he added, "We will land in the valley below the gates of the city."

She watched while Deem began to turn *Dara.* He pushed a pedal mounted near the deck and slowly turned the steering bars to the right."

"Be gentle," said Captain Shar.

"My Second," he added to Celi, "needs to treat her like she is a woman."

Deem laughed. "I know, Captain."

"You do? Then how do you explain that landing back there? We bounced."

"Well, Captain..."

"No, you do not explain. Not to me."

Celi began to back out of the cabin. She knew the two pilots were intense in their operation of this great vehicle of the sky. When Deem turned his head Celi saw deep red in his cheek.

'He is embarrassed,' she thought as she left and closed the cabin door.

Chapter 13

Celi was pleasantly surprised at the South Gate of Salem. When they landed in the valley Captain Shar sent Deem as escort with Char and Seth acting as guards. The two men wore the *Dara's* entire allotment of side pistols in leather holsters. Deem and the two 'guards' walked up the hill with Celi behind. At the gate they were challenged.

"And you are?" asked the gate sentry.

"I am Deem, Pilot Second of the *Dara* which you just saw coming down into your filthy trash laden valley."

"And what is your business in Salem?"

"We intend to see the Vizier of King Shamash."

"Oh, I doubt you will see him."

Deem appeared to be puzzled. He looked down at his finely polished boots then up at the sentry. "You do not understand," he remarked. "This is the Lady Celiste of the royal family of Eridu that will see the Vizier."

The sentry looked at Deem then bent to his right to look around Deem at Celi. He straightened up and stepped back and waved them through.

Walking away Celi said to Deem, "I am impressed. You know who I am."

What happened next was recorded on a clay tablet found in a storage room in the 'palace' of the Vizier. Celi had been assigned a task; the task was approved by no less than Lord Enki. And yet, the Vizier of King Shamash tried to predict Celi could not succeed.

Celi left the southern gate and began walking up a well-worn path (it could not be called a road). Celi saw old one story buildings and an occasional two story with a shop facing the path. She saw piles of trash. She knew Salem was not an old town. From the sky she saw the walls around the city. She knew they would walk up hill to get to the 'palace' of the Vizier which stood in front of the King's temple. They crossed a wider road that served as a market place for farmers and butchers. They skirted around a well where six women waited to draw water. They walked around a pile of stones being used to build a wall. A dog came to investigate and Char tried to kick it but missed.

Up ahead behind the Vizier's palace they saw the round dome of the King's temple. Beyond it stood the elevated plaza built with enormous stone slabs that was used as a place of landing. When the shuttle *Dara* came down Celi saw a larger shuttle was using the landing field. Deem told her, quietly and with pride, the larger shuttle could hold 40 to 50 persons. "That is the *Cead,*" he said. "The name means 'One'." [End Note 9]

As they approached the Vizier's palace they were again challenged. This time a sentry went ahead to advise those in the palace that a royal personage was entering.

As they entered Celi suddenly felt cooler air. She walked to a railing and looked down into a black hole. There were no lights, only the cool air flowing up to her level then whisking into the building. The faint sound of water lapping the side of the wall far below came to her mind.

"What do you think, Deem?"

She turned to find they were down the hall. A large mural covered the wall opposite her. It depicted sailing ships in battle. Three flaming spheres were falling from the skies toward the 'enemy' ships. She walked to the next mural where a painter was adding dark red to the muscular chest of a horse. Steam poured from the horse's nostrils. Its rider wore a conical helmet with horns and padded wraps on his arms. One arm was straight out holding a bow while his other hand pulled a leather cord back. Some men with axes and lances were running at him.

"That is our lord, Shamash," said a man at her side.

She turned to see a man with brown hair and a long beard standing with his hands in a peak, as if he was asking Celi for something.

"The Vizier awaits you in his meeting room."

Celi followed the man through a pair of doors that were one and a half times her height. The doors were cedar; the carvings were of black mahogany against the red of the cedar. Inside she found walls covered in murals that seemed to tell of battles led by Shamash. There were servants behind the Vizier; they were the brown-haired men and women Celi thought of as *Beag*, which meant 'short, strong.'

The small crowd parted as she and Deem approached. Char and Seth took up stations near the doors, as they had seen others do. What they saw was impressive. A platform sat at the end of the long narrow room. An old man dressed in long robes sat on a throne. His head wore a cloth cap of green linen with gold threads. He held the scepter of power. His nose was large and bent. His face carried valleys of sadness, yet there were smiles in the corner of his mouth.

The Vizier raised his hand and beckoned Celi to come forward. She walked to the platform edge with Deem behind her.

"State your position," said the man.

"I am Celi, granddaughter of Lady Ningal at Ur."

That is sufficient. I know of you," remarked the old man.

"You are?" he aimed at Deem.

"Deem, Pilot Second of the *Dara*."

"You I have no knowledge of."

"I am the lady's escort."

"Ah, I see." The Vizier motioned for the people around him to leave the long hall. While they moved away he motioned to a young girl. She wore black trousers under a short white tunic that had been cleaned and pressed. Her brown hair was cut with bangs across her forehead that partially hid her distinctive brow ridge.

The servant brought a tray with small bowls. She allowed Celi and Deem to take a bowl off the tray. She began to turn away then touched the cloth of Celi's robe. Celi looked down in surprise.

The Vizier exploded. He jumped up and reached for a short rod that had strips of leather attached. He swung the device and it cracked against the girl's back.

"You have been warned," he shouted.

The woman cringed. She straightened her back against the pain.

"You 'Brown Hairs' need to learn your place in my world." The old man swung the whip again. It cracked against her back.

He began to swing again. In a blur of motion Deem slid around Celi and placed himself between the old man and the girl. The old man was slow to react. Deem caught the whip and stopped it. The girl took three steps away from the Vizier, turned and said, "Thank you."

The mighty Vizier looked at Deem's hand on his whip and backed away. The whip dropped on the floor. He snarled and said, "You … girl …what do you say?"

She looked puzzled. She said nothing.

"They are slow," he said to Deem and shouted, "Thank you, my lord!" at the girl.

From the back of the room a man approached, took the girl by the arm and walked her out. The guard was smiling in anticipation of privately punishing the girl. The Vizier went across the platform and lowered himself onto an ornate chair with an enormous pillow. His face displayed a look of disgust.

Without so much as a pause the Vizier asked, "What is it you ask of me?"

Celi was mute, her mind a fuzz of reactions. She began then stopped.

"My lady asks not for herself, but for her village of Arad," said Deem. There was color in his face; he seemed angry.

"Can she not speak?" snarled the old man.

Deem turned around to face the entry door. He motioned to one of his 'guards' to come forward. When Char reached him Deem retrieved Char's pistol and turned around to face the Vizier.

He looked at the pistol and caressed the barrel. Then he looked up and shouted, "Where did you learn to disrespect my lady?"

The thin white eyebrows on the old man went up. He was focused on the pistol in Deem's hand. He started to rock in his chair, and then held up a hand.

"I did not…"

"You swung that whip next to my lady Celiste."

"So?"

"You broke the bonds of our society. No one makes offensive actions near a lady and then you shouted almost directly at her."

"She should know," the man stammered.

"She should know what?" snarled Deem.

"She goes on a task with no reward."

"How do you mean?"

"The women in that village are 'Brown-Hairs' who will not survive."

"How is that?"

"They cannot learn."

"How do you know this?"

"The sister of King Shamash is at Arad, for two months now."

"And?" asked Celiste, finally clearing her head.

"She tells the King that the crops are planted but the women do not seem to care about working in the fields."

"So," began Deem slowly while he tucked the pistol into his wide belt, "you do not believe Lady Celiste can do anything to help them learn?"

The Vizier was silent, as if he suddenly realized he was on thin ground, that insulting the capabilities of a Princess was not a wise action.

Celi told the Vizier that she would remember the insults. In the end he agreed to send two wagons, four horses, a windmill and water pump, and four fish nets. The girl who touched Celi would be sent to Arad with the wagons. Seth would be left behind to escort the girl and two 'Brown-haired' men who knew horses.

After his agreement Celi bowed low to the Vizier and her chin jutted out. "You will be surprised. We will survive." Celi and Deem backed away from the Vizier as required by court protocol and left the fancy hall.

Coming down the path toward *Dara* she said, "You surprised me."

"How, my lady?"

"You stood up to the most powerful man in this region."

"Captain Shar warned me."

Behind her she heard Char stumbling over rocks. They were crossing bumpy ground strewn with rocks. She smiled. Then she reached over and placed her hand under Deem's arm.

Chapter 14

Dara was briefly above the clouds on the flight south from Salem. In the clouds Celi saw bumpy flowing hills and brilliant white color. Captain Shar found a hole in the clouds and down they came, right on top of the White Sea. He explained it was a source of salt shipped to Salem then east to Eridu and Ur. He tilted *Dara* so Celi could see the flat white expanse below them. Then he pointed to the west and said, "Arad is in the shadows of those mountains." [End Note 10]

Celi saw brown rock and black shadows of mountains. They flew down a valley; sharp angular cliffs passed by. Then a small village appeared. Deem turned and pointed down. Celi saw a few roofs and many shells of houses without roofs. She thought, *'What happened?'*

Shar flew them on a circular route. In the late afternoon sunlight, she saw brief outlines of buildings on the edges of a wide, flat river. They flew out across the fields. There were long rows of young plants. Celi saw green fields that were divided by small canals of water. She saw two women working in one field. There was no sign of the other women.

Shar turned *Dara* in a loop to the north. He explained he was lining up to land on the road that ran north from near the village. Shar made her return to her seat. Then he yelled, "It will be bumpy. This road has ruts."

She felt two struts hit the surface. For a moment she had the sensation of floating as they bounced upward. They seemed to fly again before the *Dara* again set her struts on the road, which was followed by a loud bang. The steering rockets went quiet. There was a grinding from the struts crunching on old gravel and the shuttle went quiet.

They waited a few minutes. Celi knew they waited for any dust to blow away from the *Dara.* The rear hatch opened. Deem came from in front and announced, "We are down. Please accept my apologies for the manner in which we landed."

In the back Char snorted and added, "You like to throw fear into our minds."

Harn took one step toward him and said, "Close your mouth."

Gran stepped around him and looked past Celi at the old village and its mud-brick houses.

Deem waved a hand at Seth, Dana and Char and said "We are down. Get your gear and exit. Check for threats."

Celi frowned at this and then she understood. It was procedure.

She stepped to the top of the ramp where she saw empty houses and a large tower in its midst. Several women appeared from around a corner. No one appeared to be ready for her arrival.

She saw square boxes built with mud bricks; a few had a window to one side of the empty door. On higher ground she saw flat white limestone on the face of a building. There was a circular tower at one corner. A cloth of two colors, red and white, hung from a pole at the roof of the temple. Below the banner she saw a woman standing on a flat roof. The woman turned and disappeared into the temple.

She sensed Deem standing behind her. “This is your village. You must walk in as if the Lord Enlil himself has sent you.”

“In a way, he has, or his brother Enki has,” she noted. “I must, you say?”

“Use your rank.”

She smiled. “From now on you are Deem.”

Her comment drew a blank face. Then he said, “As you wish.”

“How far is the lake I saw?”

“About two days walking,” said Deem, and then added, “It is called Yām ha-Māret, but some say ‘Sea of Death.’ It is not healthy.”

“And these broken down relics?”

“The village was Arad two hundred years in the past …abandoned during a flood.”

Captain Shar stepped up behind Deem and Celi and added, “Your task is to grow beans, onions, radishes and lettuce for Hebron, where they send it north to Salem.”

She turned to look toward the fields. She saw green fields with tender shoots bending in a soft breeze. At the edge of one field there was a crew of four women working. Their legs were bare; their short tunics were hiked up to their waists. They were ‘planting’ tubes that brought water over small dikes, into the fields. *‘They control how much water, I think.’*

She looked at Captain Shar. “And you?” she said quietly.

“We return in four days. *Dara* goes to get more workers, all women, for this village.”

Celi glanced at Deem. She saw him raise an eyebrow. He smiled.

“It’s only four days,” added Deem. “Time enough for you to get settled.”

‘And prepare for your arrival?’ she thought but said aloud, “You seem to have a high opinion of yourself Pilot Deem.”

He looked startled for a moment. "Your wish is my…" he began before Captain Shar remarked, "Lady Celiste is tired. Get this man to take her gear."

Deem said nothing. He turned and motioned to Char, "Lady Celi expects to show her rank. Carry her bags."

Char nodded and re-entered for Celiste's clothing. Dana came off *Dara* with the two rifles and her clothes bag. She gave one rifle to Seth and held the second. Char came down the ramp and said with a smirk, "Yes, my lady?"

Chapter 15

They stepped off *Dara's* ramp and walked toward the village. Deem came first with a side arm inside a leather strap. He wore his formal red uniform with the seven-pointed star on his tunic. Behind him Char brought Celi's two bags of possessions. Dana and Seth were left behind to guard *Dara.* Celi came last; she wore a red tunic over her long white gown. Her hair was wrapped in a red and white cloth that fell to her shoulders.

They walked up a well-trodden path that led from the fields to the houses of Arad. Celi looked down when she realized some of the fine dirt was inside her toes. From between the houses two men with short curved swords appeared. Then a woman with the regal bearing of the Aryas followed. She was dressed in a short wrap that reached her knees. Her hair was pulled back and protected by a long swatch of cloth wound around her head. She had the straight nose, black hair and high cheekbones of the Aryas. She did not smile.

When she stopped the two men in front of her stopped. They stepped to both sides of the path. Deem and his entire party separated into two lines. This left Celi in mid-path, directly opposite the other woman.

Deem made a small bow in the woman's direction and swung an arm wide, pointing vaguely in Celi's direction. "Lady, I have the honor to…"

"Yes," said the woman.

"Pree…sent…" he tried.

"Yes," said the woman.

"Lady 'Say-Leest-Ay' who is…"

"Yes," repeated the lady.

Deem stopped. He stood straight and turned to look sideways at Celi. She minutely raised an eyebrow and cleared her throat.

"I am…"

The lady ignored her and turned to Deem. "Are you the pilot?"

Deem turned away from the lady. Celi unbuttoned her long coat and exposed her silver medallion, her emblem of rank. To the lady she said,

"He is the pilot."

"Then he should know that I will retrieve my maids, my clothes and leave."

"With my permission," stated Celi with blunt authority.

The woman looked at Celi, then at Deem and said, "I was told 30 days in this dismal place. It has been 57. I am ready to leave."

"You will leave when I grant you the right to leave," said Celi with a certain amount of hot pepper inside her voice.

The lady looked stunned. She said nothing.

"You are?"

"Gebi, a daughter of Salem, our glorious center of knowledge."

"From what I saw your center of knowledge is a trash heap." Celi waited for a reaction but there was none.

"And your role here in Arad?"

"Directing the rebuilding. We made no progress."

"And why are you proud of, as you say *no progress*?"

"These women have no pride, no sense of purpose."

"Explain please," said Celi in two words of a demand.

Lady Gebi looked down at her feet for a moment and seemed to guess she was making a Princess with rank stand in the sun. Her voice went up with urgency when she said, "Please. I am solely aggrieved that you stand here. Come into your temple. My maids will wash your feet."

"Explain yourself," repeated Celi.

The lady looked away. She glanced at Celi's helpers and waved them toward the white stone temple. To Deem she said, "My lord?"

"I will stand with Lady Celi," said Deem.

"Explain yourself," Celi said once again.

"You must understand. I take responsibility for my failure," said Gebi while she looked boldly into Celi's eyes. "There was a full squad of men here. They planted the onions and beans and radishes that this dismal hovel will send to Hebron and Salem. An old shipment of barley seed went into the ground. No lettuce. The men planned to grind and ferment the barley. Two of the men joined with our women. The rest, shall I say, were of a lustful nature and abused our women. They were all taken away to serve in the Army of Enlil."

Celi said nothing.

"We have struggled to prepare your quarters. The washing pool is clean and your quarters are private. An old woman prepares our food. I have dismissed the two priests who were making a shambles of the temple."

"And where do the workers sleep?"

"Three of the old ruins have been dug out. There was one cubit of dirt and debris inside the ruins. We were about to build roofs when the men were taken. The fields are growing. My half-sister waters the fields."

"But you have done little to repair the small hovels?"

"Yes, my lady," said Lady Gebi.

"You will stay. You and your maids can serve me for the next ten days. We will make progress in building roofs or you will stay longer. Am I making myself like a crystal that shines beyond doubt?"

The lady said nothing. She busied herself brushing imaginary dust off her gown. She nodded at her two guards then led Celi and Deem into the old streets of Arad and to the temple.

Chapter 16

The reflection off the distant lake was brilliant and blinding, a white hot beam of sunlight reflected off the water of the lake in the early morning. The fields in front of Arad were quiet. In the hour before dawn a misty dew settled on the plants. Each morning Celi and a few of the women walked out into the fields to feel the dew. They had never seen such a wealth of water sprinkled on the young plants, almost as if by magic.

Four days became eight. While Celi waited the horses and wagons arrived. Seth brought the young servant girl, called Sara, with two men who knew horses. Celi's friends Gran and Harn organized teams to build roofs on the old shells of houses. Gran and Eglan, the half-sister of Gebi, insisted on an afternoon review, when the squad leaders reported on the day's progress and plans for the next day. Celi found herself in an unusual situation: when the squad leaders asked for a day of rest, Celi was firm in her determination to continue building roofs.

The squad leader in the fields, Eglan, began to train workers in how to 'gently' water the raised fields. She explained how the canals had to be cleaned. She demanded that one worker be present to monitor the tubes used to drain excess water from the low side of the fields. She led teams with chopping sticks to clean the vagrant plants that always grew inside the row crops like radishes and onions.

"They enjoy this work ...out in the fields," Eglan commented.

Celiste watched the 'field squad' walk past on their way to the washing house. They all smiled at the *new* 'Lady' of Arad.

"Why do they smile?"

"They stand on their feet, unlike in the temple at Salem." Eglan smiled at the last woman passing by and waved her on to the washing house.

"These are temple women?" Celiste's jaw dropped.

"They earned much in tribute for the temple," began Eglan. "But you know they provided a service to men?"

"This is new to me," said Celiste.

"They were promised men," said Eglan.

"What? ...here? Instead they find an almost abandoned village, the men removed?" said Celiste in disbelief.

"They held a lottery for the two guards."

"So you will tell me two of the women are happier than the other three?"

"Yes, my Lady."

"And Lady Gebi's maids?"

"My sister has rank in the temple. Her maids are each a priestess in their own right. They have mates."

"Their mates are not here?"

"No. But by custom the absent priestess must assign a slave to service her mate."

"So the priestess assigns an ugly slave?"

Eglan stood for a moment. A frown formed on her face. She looked at Lady Celiste, then up at the white stone of the temple. One eyebrow seemed to droop as comprehension dawned across her face.

"We did not have slaves," noted Celiste.

"How did you…?"

"Each male was required to have a mate by the end of his eighteenth year."

"What about unmarried females?"

"They joined their sisters as 'Wife Number Two' and the problem was solved."

"I think you tease me?" asked Eglan.

"Oh?"

"We have no ugly slaves," noted Eglan with an enormous grin.

When Celi asked about Eglan's title, Lady Gebi went into great details to describe her two brothers and four sisters. Eglan was the last-born girl; she was almost a slave to the rest of the family.

Seven days passed. Most of day eight was filled with field work. Lady Gebi and her maids built a platform and 'created' a sleeping pad for Celi's bedroom. Her two guards were adamant they were not wood-workers; they spent their time shaping wood for the roofs on the 'hovels' as Celi called them. Celi, by her own admission, was worried. Four days had stretched to eight. She wondered about the *Dara*. She studied the skies and waited.

Late on the eighth day when the sun began to fall into the mountains to the west, the *Dara* came with a loud scream down a nearby gorge. She blasted past the small village and flew half-way to the lake. She circled to the north, approached the old road and landed in a whirlwind of dust. After her engines were quiet the ramp dropped. A long minute passed then Deem appeared. Behind him came a line of women with small bags of possessions.

Celi and Gran watched the women walk toward the village. Last to step off *Dara* were a man and woman who, as it happened, was Char's brother Marl and his mate Melan. They carried bags for clothes and a fishnet. Char stepped around Celi, bowed to the two women and went to greet his brother. The two men stopped in front of Celi and Gran and made a small bow.

"You honor us. We received training," Marl said and added, "We are beyond belief happy …" he paused, "…to be off *Dara.*"

Celi looked at Deem and said, "Pilot, you are here."

"I am," he remarked with a small bow. Then he added, "I am now Captain Deem. "We went to Abzu, the gold mines. Marl and his mate asked to be assigned as guards. The lady told me to take them to you."

"Your Captain said four days," Celi commented.

"We were directed to the highlands. We made long trips to bring 36 'Brown-haired Beag' to the army. You are expected in Salem tomorrow." End Note 11

"I am?" she asked then said, "I will take my assistant," to which Deem nodded.

"And so eight days passed," remarked Celi before she realized her comment might sound as if she missed Deem in those eight days.

"The Lady who directs the mines had your request. 'They will be trained', she said." Deem gestured toward Marl and Melan and noted they received training with a rifle and with fish nets. "They were already experienced hunters."

"You are welcome in Arad," said Celi.

"This village needs guards against deserters from the army," noted Deem.

"And protection from ourselves," added Celi.

"Only if the Lady tells you to use your weapon," added Gran.

Char and Marl and his mate Melan, who stood three paces behind them, made a thin bow and said in unison, "It shall be as our lady wishes."

Celi raised her right fist as symbol and stated: "The Lady Celi declares 'Let no guard use a rifle unless directed.' Let no man say otherwise."

She then touched Gran on the arm and indicated it was time to walk to the temple. As Celi turned away from Deem she glanced at him and said, "That was four days ago?"

He smiled. He knew she would ask. Captain Shar had 'promised' four days and here it was the end of the eighth day. "We went to the highlands in the mountains, where the air is dry. We bring you the Beag who were assigned to work in the fields."

"Assigned?"

"What do you ask?"

"Assigned? I thought they were volunteers; their mates serve in the army."

"Ahhh..." he began. "I see."

"I think not," Celi said. Then she added, "I will have to personally check your eyes later," she noted with a rather large smile.

Sideways she saw a frown on Gran's face.

"Tis fine, my friend. I give him a hard time."

The new members of her squad stopped in the stone plaza in front of the temple. The women waited. Celi told them they were there to work in the fields. That meant building the hovels into useable protection from the elements, which meant roofs.

"There is a large building near the river; it is our washing house." From among the women Celi chose the oldest and gave her charge of the Washing House. "You join the other woman. When there are no females present men may receive permission."

Then she surprised the group. She asked Seth to show his rifle. He did. "This will kill at a distance," she added. No one was allowed to touch that weapon except the village guards. She thought for a moment and told the crowd that Harn was now Keeper of the Laws and Guards. She explained by saying that Harn and his guards would be expected to observe the laws. Disobedience to the laws would be punishable with the lash. Theft or rape, by death.

"Sharing your bed with any person who is not your mate will be punishable with death," she stated bluntly.

When Deem asked she told him a few of the women had encouraged 'evil' behavior. Deem chuckled and said, "Like your ancestors who came and 'knew' the daughters of Earth?"

"My ancestors were not *'mated'* to those women, were they?"

"No, I imagine they were not."

Celi stood and watched Gran assign the women to sleeping quarters. She heard Gran accuse them of being dirty. Gran told them to head for the washing house. As the women moved away Gran said, "Their clothes are rags. We need long tunics."

Char and his brother Marl turned for the men's quarters. Celi watched them walk away. Later that evening Celi sent her servant to invite Deem to her table. The old lady who cooked for Lady Gebi and Celi prepared mutton and fish and onions. Lady Gebi was absent with a crew building sleeping platforms.

"That man Marl has a mate," said Deem after he sat in the large chair at her table.

"And you wonder?"

"Will he meet his mate in a quiet corner of this village?"

"That is for them to decide," said Celi.

Deem picked up a three-pronged fork and speared a piece of mutton. He brought it up to his nose and sniffed. He looked directly at Celi and asked, "Your rule about sharing your bed. You do not expect all these women to stay away from the men do you?"

"That is the point of the rule. There are four un-mated men. Do you see?"

"Yes, perhaps, and thirty women."

Celi saw the color coming into his face and thought, *'Perhaps Pilot Deem you have memories of your own?'*

"You mentioned our ancestors who came to Eridu and Ur and Lagash and 'visited' with some of the Beag women." [End Note 12]

Deem looked at her. "I did not mean to insult your grandfathers."

"No, no," she said quickly. "I meant did you ever?"

"You mean did I ever?"

"Did you, you know, have a friend among the Beag?"

"That I visited? You mean?"

Celi stopped. She could feel that she had crossed an invisible barrier. This line of questions would never help their relationship, if there was to be one.

"You are testing me, my lady?"

Celi lowered her face to look at her hands. "I am sorry."

Deem coughed, and then cleared his throat. He took out a thin white cloth and blew his nose. "Do you wonder why I did not?"

He paused. "Shall we say, visit?" *Do you know I was ordered to touch no women?*

When she was silent he added, "I did not have an urge."

"And now you do, have the urge, I mean?"

"You are somehow turning my words back on me," he said.

"You must have no worry in that area." Celi laughed and stood up. "You seem honorable but a little full of yourself." she added with a smile.

"I can hope we are friends," he said quietly, as Harn approached.

"We are," she said, "or *shall be,"* she said in a soft voice.

Chapter 17

The valley at Salem seemed to be cleaner. Celi, escorted by Gran and Captain Deem, was surprised to be met at the gate by an escort of four men. As she walked uphill to the Lord's temple she could not have imagined how her life would change.

At the door to the temple two slaves dressed in long white robes brought a red robe to her. One helped her wrap the robe around her. A long white banner was placed around her neck so it fell across her chest. At her shoulder the banner carried a square cross, the symbol of King Anu's reign. An aide appeared and instructed Gran to sit in the back of the room where a section was reserved for witnesses.

In the center of the Great Hall of Justice a single slab of stone was supported by two wide legs of stone. The edge of the altar had been carved smooth with symbols. There were embers in the bowl of the altar and the smell of pungent herbs inside the hall. The aide stood behind Celi and Deem while she explained the symbols were the names of King Anu and his children Enlil, Enki, and Ninĝarsag. The herbs, she added, were to mask the smell of some of the 'unwashed' visitors. [End Note 13]

Chairs were stationed in a semi-circle facing the front of the altar. Most were filled by observers. Beyond the altar was a raised platform; a row of twelve chairs spread across the platform. Ten chairs were filled with persons of high rank wearing white banners with stitched red crosses at the bottom edge. Several aides were standing around talking among themselves. The aide behind Celi coughed to get Celi's attention and pointed at an empty chair. She told Deem to find a space behind the row of twelve chairs.

Celi walked slowly. She was aware that Lord Enki sat in the center seat. Next to him sat his mate Ninki. Celi had been told the old mistress would be present. She was lost in a nap. When Celi sat next to her Ninki woke up and smiled. She waved at an aide who came quickly to help her rise. When she was standing the aide offered her his arm but she pushed him off.

"I rise to..." she began then paused. "Oh, yes. This is Celiste, granddaughter of Ningal and entitled to sit while Ningal is absent at the mines."

"What do I do?" said Celi when Ninki sat down.

"Nothing. Listen."

Celi looked around the enormous hall. Long columns supported the dome and the roof. Beyond the columns were flat walls with images of warriors in battle, farmers behind plows, workers tending fields, and a man with a tube on a tripod under dark skies. Over to her left she saw a scribe with his table. Behind him stood the Vizier of Shamash looking as officious as ever, decked out in long robes with a red banner across his chest. There were several other men with red sashes but she did not know who they were.

The doors opened with a squeal. Outside Celi saw three men waiting to enter. While they waited a priest in a long robe came to the altar and placed herbs on the embers. Lazy white smoke rose toward the dome. A servant stepped into the doorway and raised a ram's horn to his lips. His blast on the horn certified there were no 'half-asleep' witnesses present.

The three men entered the Great Hall. Their leader wore a long white robe stained with mud on its hem. He wore a silver medallion of the 'thick' cross. Celi realized this man was a 'priest' of considerable influence.

The 'priest' walked to the altar and placed a small branch of acacia on the embers. He leaned over the altar to get a whiff of the light green smoke.

The priest bowed to Lord Enki and waited. Several moments later Enki raised a hand in a gesture that said 'Proceed.'

"My Lord," he began. "Those were acacia flowers. To help me see the future."

Lord Enki smiled.

"But like most things of this world, they do not provide answers."

There was a murmur among the crowded observers. Celi heard two people mumbling behind her. Lady Ninki patted Celi's arm, as if to say, 'Be patient.'

Lord Enki stood and announced, "Listen to the words of Abram. This is Abram, he who defeated the Hittite kings and now prepares to do battle with Mar.Duk."

Enki made a small bow towards Abram and added, "Of course, you were younger in those days."

Abram made a shallow bow toward Lord Enki. "My family fled Ur and fled the tyranny of their king after he defeated Lagash. I was young when I defeated the four kings at Damascus. I am still young."

Lady Ninki snorted and said, "You are? Your wrinkles echo mine. We are neither of us very young."

Enki laughed, then nodded and said, "You bring us news?"

"My men captured an officer of Mar.Duk's army south of Babylon."

"What news did he bring?"

"Mar.Duk builds his army to capture Tilmun."

"How do you know this?" asked Lady Ninki.

"He told us."

"How did you get him to tell you?"

"We pressured him."

"How did you pressure him?" asked Ninki.

When the priest/general Abram stalled, the lady added, "You think me incapable of holding the truth if you tell me? Do not mistake my age for incompetence."

Abram bowed. "Forgive me, my lady," he said quietly. "I serve."

"Answer my question," she said in a firm voice.

"We pressure our guests by stretching their arms between two posts. They hang in the air; their feet cannot touch the ground."

"And then?"

"We convince them to tell us what they know."

"Is that all?"

"We threaten to cut off their male member."

Lady Ninki was silent. She looked at Celi then at the other two women present. A minute passed. She looked back at General Abram and asked, "Where is this officer now?"

"His head, my lady, is on a pole in front of my tent."

There was a gasp among the observers. Celi heard a grunt from behind her.

Two of the men sitting to the right of Lord Enki stood up. One of them was clearly upset. He sat down. The other man said, "Did you consider alternatives?"

"My camp is large. We train many officers and multitudes of 'brown-haired' recruits that need to have lessons about my discipline in the camps."

There was silence. Lord Enki stood and said "Thank you. Your message is received."

Chapter 18

"He asked for the Council to approve a war," said Celi to Deem. "There was no decision."

"There can be no decision until twelve are present." Celi explained what Lady Ninki said as the Council began to leave. They stood off to the side when the Lady asked for a quiet conference with Celi and 'her' Captain.

"The royals seem to glory in their titles and descendant position from Anu," said Celi.

Deem glanced at Celi. "Perhaps we should not be critical."

"Perhaps?" What Celi thought to herself was, *'Perhaps you should not be in awe of persons who allow warriors to behead their enemies or who allow slaves to live in squalid conditions.'*

As the temple emptied Celi heard Lady Ninki say, "Can you believe it?"

When they said nothing, she repeated herself. "Can you believe it?"

Her minister finally interjected and said softly, "Say 'No, mistress'." He brought a hand up and pointed at his ear, telling them Ninki had a problem hearing.

"No, mistress," said Deem loudly.

"So short, I say. No one around here pays me any attention," Ninki said loudly to her minister before she turned to Celi and Deem. "There was a time when our sons were two heads taller than…" she began but her head seemed to acquire a bouncing rhythm of its own.

Her minister stepped to her side and presented a papyrus scroll. He then unrolled it and said, "Captain Deem, the rank of your mate Celi is confirmed. Her assignment is to direct a crops operation with 40 workers. Lord Enki confirms the appointment of Deem to the rank of Captain of the *Dara*."

Deem suddenly stood up taller. His face acquired a blank expression. He began to say, "But Lady Celiste is not my…"

But the minister interrupted. "We are finished. My Lady has signed this decree."

Lady Ninki motioned for Celi to approach.

"How do you say it?"

"My Lady?"

"Your name, dear."

"Ah, my grandfather preferred 'Say-Leest-Ay.'

"Thank you." She sat and looked around to her minister.

"What was it?" she said loudly. He bowed, slightly.

"Tilmun," he said equally loudly.

Lady Ninki turned to Celi and said slowly, with great pauses in her words: "Tilmun …Land of the Missiles …a dangerous place …you will be far north of Tilmun …near the deep lake they call White Sea. Listen to me, my dear."

Celi turned her ear toward Lady Ninki; she indicated she was listening. A small frown formed on her face.

"Mar.Duk, at Babylon, is tired of the desert and the palms and the big river. He wants to build a temple; he has taken possession of Eridu."

Celi stood; her mind turned fuzzy *'Mica, my Mica. He is working for Mar.Duk?'* Then she realized her grandfather, at his age, might not have survived the invasion of Mar.Duk's troops.

Ninki reached out to touch Celi's arm. "There will be war," the old lady said slowly. "Mar.Duk refuses to retreat from Eridu. General Abram's army is growing. Mar.Duk is building an army. Some of your people have joined with the Army of Abram."

Celi nodded and said she agreed with 'my Lady.'

The old lady nodded, once. Then she looked at Celi and said, "What name did your grandmother have?"

"Misha Leone, we called her Misha," answered Celi.

"Good. If you get a message from Misha Leone, then move your people into the mountains." The old lady paused then said, "Do you understand?"

"You honor me, Lady."

"Do you understand?"

Celi bowed and said, "I understand." The old lady crooked a finger at Celi and urged her to come closer. When Celi was close Lady Ninki handed her a silver ankh, the oval circle on the top of the 'T' that once represented the great island that was flooded when the stars fell. [End Note 14]

Celi looked at the medallion. "Does it represent...?"

"It was a city on a plain near the shore of the Great Western Sea. Just beyond the tall rock faces some call 'pillars.' They built two canals around the raised hill; they were a seafaring people. Until their land flooded and the survivors came to Enoch's pyramid near the Great Lion.

"It is a mark of trust in your position."

"Wear this symbol when next you meet with the Council."

"Yes, my lady."

"This young man? This Deem?"

"Yes?"

"Latch onto him. Do not allow other women to go fishing."

Celi said nothing.

"There are women who know how to become bait for such a handsome fish."

The old lady smiled and laughed. Her laugh turned into a rasp and she coughed. Her right hand waved Celi away. Her Vizier, from behind Lady Ninki, bowed toward Celi and waved his hand to indicate it was appropriate to leave his mistress' presence.

As they walked out of the temple Deem asked, "And that was…?"

"Just talk between the two of us," began Celi. "She seems to think you would make a good…" But she paused. And remembered Mica's proverb, *'Those who think the fish is large are usually disappointed.'*

Chapter 19

The sun continued to climb into the northern hemisphere while the plants reached maturity. When it became evident the radishes and onions needed to be harvested, Gran reported a wagon and two of the pulling beasts was needed. Lady Gebi also noted the need for salt and meat.

Celi considered their request for a moment then said, "We only planted one crop each year. The cold made it difficult to get a whole crop. We never even asked about a second crop."

"In this land, two crops in most years," said Lady Gebi.

"How do you know?" said Celi, perhaps without thinking.

"All my life I have lived in Salem. My older brothers served on the gates as guards. When I visited them we talked about what was entering and leaving each day."

"My brothers always took a few of each crop as tribute to the city. In quiet moments we ate what we had."

Gebi stopped and looked out over the fields. Gran turned and walked toward the washing house. Gebi turned to Celi and said quietly,

“You must remember. You are Aryas. You know these things. Do not, and I repeat, do not query a royal ever in front of the Beag. We hold high status because we know the answers and the magic and the style of our ships and our tablets.” Gebi finished her comment and raised an eyebrow, as if asking for agreement.

“Yes,” said Celi. Her cheeks felt warm. *‘This woman has the onions to give me directions? She is nothing but a dried radish.’* She enjoyed the comparison. *‘I will say nothing.’*

Gebi glanced at Celi and added, “We cannot and do not trust the Beag. We are Aryas. We are pure. They are not. They are the unlawful children of our Lords and our, how shall I say this? …our brothers and cousins who like to dally with the daughters of Earth.”

‘They are not that different,’ added Celi to herself.

The sun was high overhead when Harn walked back into the plaza near the temple. His clothes were dirty with dust and mud. He was followed by two Beag, Char and his brother Marl. Char carried a rifle strapped to his back. Marl had a bundle tied to his back and he turned toward the river and the ‘old’ cook house.

“We found deep red beets up in the higher lands,” Harn told Celi while she watched Marl walk toward the house they repaired, with the tall brick chimneys. A light current of pale smoke drifted upward from the two chimneys of the cooking house.

Celi looked at the dirt on Harn’s face and smiled. His tunic and trousers were covered in pale brown dust. His boots were equally dirty. Char stood tall with his rifle and said nothing.

“What is your report?” she said to Harn.

"As you asked, we found a large cave. It is in a higher valley that requires climbing. We saw a large cat in the area. The cave showed evidence of small bones. The cat lives there."

"And water?"

"There is a fast moving flow within quick walking of the cave." He hesitated then added, "The stream becomes a pool just beyond the cave then drops over a rock cliff."

Celi nodded her head. She looked at the bag of red beets and said, "Can we plant them?"

"I will ask the old caretaker," he remarked.

Celi decided to take action. To Harn and Char she said,

"Go to the cook house and eat. Tomorrow you both will escort Lady Gebi to that large village called Hebron. We need two pulling beasts, salt and one plow and seed for onions and radishes."

Harn's jaw dropped slightly. He stood there for a moment.

"Lady Gebi is going to pay a tribute to Arad, our village. Her tribute will be two horses, salt, a plow and more seed and a four-legged meat animal."

"In return for what?"

"You will haul the Lady and her two maids and our first load of radishes to Salem. She will not return with you."

Char snorted. He turned away from Celi and Harn. His shoulders bounced, as if he laughed.

"And you two," snarled Celi, "will never present yourself to me or any other royal in this condition, ever. If you do, I shall have you whipped."

Harn looked at her with a blank face.

"And you, Char. You have had your hands on one of Lady Gebi's maids two or three times. You will stop such behavior. This is your only warning. You are demoted. Give the rifle to your brother, and tell him my order. Perhaps he can keep you out of my anger."

Harn and Char stood for a moment with blank faces. Harn began to bow toward 'Lady' Celi. Char followed suit. Celi turned and walked into the temple; she began to think of it as 'her' temple.

Chapter 20

D*ara* returned. Celi walked out to meet Captain Deem. After the dust blew away the ramp came down. Deem appeared in the doorway. Celi immediately thought, *Strange. He never smiles.*

Then she realized he wore his working uniform with the Captain's emblem of rank on his right shoulder. *He is not going to stay?*

Even before he reached her Deem began to shout. "We saw a camp of refugees west of Eridu. We were scouting to see if Mar.Duk had advanced beyond Eridu."

"And your report?"

Deem's smile faded. "No advance."

He looked into her eyes and could see she was puzzled. She dressed in her white 'work' tunic and sandals. There were smudges of dirt on her face. There was a deep brown of mud on one knee. The front of her tunic was damp. He could almost see the charms of her breasts. He began to smile, and said "I want to put my arms around you."

"What?"

He stopped and looked at Celi. "Did I just say...?"

"Yes, your arms around me?

Celi took a step back. She tried to gather her thoughts. Was Deem just impertinent or was he always this way, not afraid to seduce a woman? "I cannot believe..."

"What I said? Deem replied. He shook his head. It was clearly time to change tactics, after all he brought great news. He saw Celi was looking at the *Dara* ramp. Her jaw dropped minutely. She began to smile and pushed herself around Deem. She moved to the bottom of the ramp and threw her arms around Mica, her grandfather.

"As I began to say, we saw this camp."

"And you brought me Mica?"

"Well ...yes," he began. He brought his hands together and made a small bow in her direction. "And two other men his age. They are stone workers."

"Yes, they are welcome."

Celi looked up the ramp. Two men in ragged long robes with cloths over their heads stood there holding small bundles of clothing. She pushed herself back from Mica and looked him over. "My eyes are pleased to see you. You need..." she said then pointed at the washing house, "...all three of you to the washing house. Wash. Then present yourself in the house with two chimneys."

She turned toward Deem. If anything his smile was wider. "Do not think you can charm me with your smile, Captain Deem."

"But?"

"I admit it. You have helped me. And you have helped Arad."

"Does that mean I am entitled to a reward?

"What would you ask?" Her face began to frown.

"I already told you."

Celi stepped away from the ramp and walked around Deem, heading for her temple. "You will join me in the cooking house for a meal, when the sun hits the top of the mountain. We worked hard today. I must wash."

Deem watched her walk toward her temple. Behind Deem the Second Pilot Aonim said, "Your reach is high. She will have your male member removed." Aonim laughed.

The day after Deem returned in *Dara* he helped the two maids to climb into the wagon among the bags of radishes. They took bags with clothes and food and Lady Gebi's formal clothes and her personal items used to prepare her face and hair. She walked onto the plaza in a long flowing cloth coat. Over the long coat she wore a short coat with a hood over her hair. Her face barely showed but the black oil on her eyelids seemed to give her a sinister appearance. Two of the guards helped her climb onto the back of the wagon.

Her maids had prepared an over-size chair with two pillows and she sat slowly down while she tested the chair. She looked regal despite being surrounded by bags of radishes. Her maids sat on top of the radishes. Harn and Marl, with his rifle on his shoulder, sat at the front of the wagon. At the last moment the old lady who cooked for Lady Gebi brought out a bundle with cooked onions, beans and the newest addition to their daily menu, a ground wheat product formed into rolls and baked.

Lady Gebi said nothing to the cook. One of her maids said, "We thank you," to which the cook replied, "Not me. Lady Celi ordered me to send this food with you."

The maid smiled. Harn raised the leather ropes on the pulling beasts and urged them to begin moving. Lady Gebi looked with disgust at the cook and said, "Perhaps someday you will learn to prepare food beyond boiling the goodness out of it."

Under her breath the cook said, "Yes, I boil, you leave." The cook smiled.

Celi was seated at a small table in the great hall of her temple. She had recently washed and wore a long white robe with her sandals. Her hair was pulled back inside a head wrap; it was her usual manner of dress. She awaited Captain Deem.

Deem had used the 'washing house' to clean himself while the women were banned. He wore a thin tunic over black trousers. His wet hair was slicked back.

Celi caught a whiff of his scent and said, "You smell like a man."

"Thank you, my lady," he responded with a slight bow from the waist. "The old lady had a ground flower she called lavender in her fire pit and when I asked she changed it to sage."

Celi glanced at his attire while she used clear oil to remove the black oil around her eyes. A shiny bronze disc on the wall served to reflect her image. She saw Deem was about to sit and decided to stand and ask,

"Will you escort me to our 'grove' outside the temple?"

"That twisted mass of date palms? Are any of them alive?"

"We are clearing it out."

"It is my task to serve," he responded ritually.

Celi began to walk toward the front gate. Deem followed, but kept himself one step back out of respect. At the large doors of the temple she stopped and said, "By my side."

"Are you sure?" he responded.

"You look so handsome," she said. To herself she added, *'And I want to show you off to these women.'*

As they approached the old grove she explained, "All the old wood is being cut for the ovens and washing house. We found young date palms and cleared around them."

She did not say she wanted to create a 'place of refuge and peace' as her grandfather Mica had chosen to do in Eridu.

In the middle of the cleared area sat a long bench made by the guards. Celi told him the guards made the bench as a gift to 'their lady' and hoped she would use it. She kicked off her sandals and sat and began to rub her calves.

Deem came around her and sat on the bench, but not close to her. He looked at Celi. She told him his behavior was appropriate. In the distance she saw Gran and Eglan arm in arm with Mica. They were passing to the cooking house but she saw them glance in her direction. *They are old friends.*

They sat quietly for some time. Deem cleared his throat but said nothing. Celi reached over and took his hand. "You are a good man."

Surprise registered on Deem's face. Without a word he swung around and went down on one knee and began to massage her calves.

She raised an eyebrow in response before she said, "Why?" and began to laugh. *'To get your hands on me?'* she chuckled to herself.

"Entirely to impress you. You must want the other women to admire and appreciate your mate. I am building your reputation."

"You are not my mate," she said.

"I know. But I have a question. Why did I bring twelve clay vessels; each amphora is one and one-half cubits tall?"

"They are going up into the mountains. They will hold water. I am preparing.

There will be a war," Celi added. "What have you heard among the Pilots?"

"Mar.Duk is building a new temple in Eridu, and Lord Enki is furious. Enki and Ninki are in Salem. Mar.Duk has caravans of wagons and men coming west. They are dragging a horde of women behind them. You know what kind of *women*; I mean?"

"Yes. It is indeed a sad thing."

Deem added that if Mar.Duk captured Tilmun he could control two of the regions, Shin'ar and Salem. He partially stood and pushed himself back onto the bench. [End Note 15]

"Should I be worried? How will I know?" Celi's face held a frown.

Deem put his hand over her hand where she had it on her leg. She looked briefly then up to his eyes before she said, "Captain Deem, stop!"

He removed his hand. He looked at his hand then moved to pick up her hand. She resisted his pull. He bent over and kissed her hand. "Know this then. If you need to leave, I will come and get you."

"Unless you are ordered ..." she began but stopped.

Chapter 21

It was the very next day that Deem fell into trouble. The trouble was, and he was not absolutely certain, but he thought he was smitten with the fair Lady Celi. When he thought about it later he claimed his trouble arose from a sense of 'here is an opportunity' and he could not help himself.

Deem and his Pilot Second, called Aonim, spent the morning hauling water from the river and washing the sides and struts of *Dara.* She shone in the mid-day light. The two aides who stood guard in the night were asleep in their bunks. It was past mid-day when Deem saw two of the Arad guards, Char and Marl walking up a slight slope that led into an old growth of heavy evergreen and ancient oak trees.

"Interesting," he said to Aonim.

He went back on board *Dara* and retrieved his side pistol from his small cabin. He buckled the belt that held the holster. His nose told him it was time to scrub down both of the small cabins used by the crew.

Coming down the ramp he passed Aonim and told him he was going to see what kind of work the two guards were doing back in the heavy woods. When he reached the edge of the trees, he paused. His nose detected the smells of wood burning and something cooking.

Cautiously he stepped into the shade of the trees. He walked slowly; he followed a twisted path between stunted oaks and around fallen giants of tree trunks. Ahead in a clearing he saw the two men. One was stirring a round copper pot. The pot sat on an iron grate above a strong fire. The other man had a drinking mug attached to an iron ladle and was using the mug to pour their 'concoction' into clay jugs.

Deem stepped into the clearing. The men did not see him at first, so he said, "It is good to see you men know how to sweat."

They straightened up from what they were doing. Marl looked down at Deem's pistol and shook his head. "Captain Deem we..."

But Char said quickly, "...found this barley the men collected before they left."

"And yeast in a cupboard in the cooking house," added Marl.

"And some apples that were going to be thrown out," said Char.

Deem laughed. "How does it taste?"

"We do not know. It makes me head fuzzy," said Marl.

"Two weeks cooking it, on and off."

"And the Lady, your mistress?"

"She believes we are burning trash. As you can see, that is true."

Deem looked at the pile of gnarled branches retrieved from the old grove. He nodded and told them the Lady Celiste should receive three jugs of their brew as tribute. They did not argue. Marl took out a knife and began to whittle stoppers for the jugs.

The women were pleased with the dresses brought back from Hebron. The cloth was woven cotton; the colors were faded. Celi was pleased but warned Harn to bring back new cloth on his next trip. They would begin to sew their clothes.

The cooking house was nearly empty. The evening meal was finished. Celi and Gran and two of her workers were chatting when Deem appeared in the door with a cloth sack over his shoulder. He nodded toward Celi and stood patiently. After a few minutes the two women stood up to head for the women's quarters.

"The washing house is mine," he said.

"And you expect me to join you?" she laughed.

"But no." He looked flustered. He could not believe that Lady Celi would treat him like so much trash.

"What is your wish, oh brave pilot of the *Dara*?" said Gran.

"I wish..." and he stopped. "There is a word?"

"To walk my lady out to her grove. I have a matter of tribute to pay to the Lady Celiste for her temple."

"The word is escort?" said Gran.

Celi laughed. "The brave pilot, as you called him, will walk me out to the grove."

"Thank you, my lady."

"When you are washed," she added.

Deem left the cooking house. He went to the washing house and asked one of the old women to soak his sack in the river while he washed. She smiled and took his sack.

The water in the washing pool was almost cool this time of day. Deem wasted no time scrubbing himself. Aonim arrived with a clean tunic and light colored, almost white trousers. He guessed Deem had something else on his mind. Deem smiled but was mute.

Deem pulled his long hair back and tied it with a cord. He found a supply of chewing sticks and cleaned his teeth. He took a small sprig of lavender and rubbed his arms with it. When he was ready he went and retrieved his bag with the three jugs.

Celi meanwhile had removed her short work tunic, washed briefly and dressed in her long white robe. She wore her red and white band around her middle. Gran helped her loosen and untangle her hair, which fell to her shoulders. She was tightening the straps of her sandals when her servant, the girl Sara, stepped into Celi's sleeping room and said, "My lady, there is a man."

"Who is the man?"

"I did not ask," said Sara.

"Tell the man I come." Celi turned to Gran as Sara left and said, "She learns but she has to be challenged."

The outer room featured a wall hanging put together by the two ladies in the washing house. They had found yellow cloth and white cloth and made a large flower that covered half of the wall. When Sara entered she said, "She comes," to Deem where he stood near the small private table.

Behind her Celi said, "Thank you, Sara," and dismissed her.

She looked at Deem with his shining hair and pleasant face and sturdy chin and his deep blue eyes and said, "You are?"

"Deem, my lady."

As Sara left the room Celi smiled. "She will know who you are. Tribute?"

"Yes. Before we walk to the grove." He patted his trousers until he found it. Deem raised the smallest little jug with a tiny stopper before her eyes.

"It is my tribute." He pulled the stopper and daubed one finger. "It is oil of myrrh." He put one drop on her neck and one drop below her chin."

"The oil of myrrh, I am told, will act as a stimulant if too much is used."

"It is good we are friends," she smiled, *'or I would have you lashed.'*

Thinking about it later, it was her actions, or rather her lack of action, that led Deem to believe she wanted to be held. In his life he had never encountered a princess who would allow another to touch her person, certainly not in public. Celi's entry room was not private; it served as a place to meet officials in semi-private. Her friend Gran was just behind her; Gran saw him touch her. Gran did not object which led Deem to believe that Gran approved.

She took the myrrh while he said, "The sun is almost down."

Celi agreed and they walked together out to the grove. She was curious about the sack he carried but waited. He put the sack on the bench and took both of her hands.

"It is time we both agree that we are friends," he said.

He pulled her to him and placed his arms around her. She bent back away from him and then she pushed him with one hand.

"That is the second time you touched me without my permission."

"Will you have me lashed, or dragged behind a horse?"

"I think lashed. I want to see you beg to be my friend."

"That would be such a noble thing to ask. Far better than being dragged."

"You think you know so much about me... I mean ...about women."

"Yes, my lady."

She had her arm straight out; her hand sat on his chest.

"What is in the bag you carried?"

"Tribute, from Marl and Char."

"Oh?"

"They have been cooking this on a fire of burning trash for two weeks."

"Yes?" she said. He opened his bag and removed one jug and gave it to her. She looked at the jug, felt its cool side and pointed it at him. "Is this good" she asked while he twisted the stopper to remove it.

"I had a taste."

She brought it up to her nose and sniffed. Her nose wrinkled. "You first."

"Yes. It is good to be cautious." He took the jug, raised it and swallowed. Both eyebrows went up. His back straightened. "Tastes of apples."

"It does?"

Celi took the jug and drank some. She thought *'this must be ale. Tis heavier than beer.'*

She turned and sat on the bench. When she looked back toward 'her temple' she saw Eglan and two of the women passing on their way to the washing house. She also saw them looking at her. *'Now the word will pass. The lady has a friend.'*

Deem sat down next to her; *'a little closer?'* she thought.

"The taste is... different." She would not tell Deem this was the first sip of alcohol she had tasted. Her grandfather Mica drank too much one night and she saw what it did to him. That night she said to him "Why?" and Mica did not have an answer.

She took another swallow. *'I could like this,'* she thought. She pointed at the bag on the bench.

"Two more," said Deem.

"Good," she said with determination. "And you?"

He turned to the bag and brought out a second jug. "What do you think?"

"Tastes like ale," she said without the faintest idea of how ale should taste. She took another swallow while he removed the stopper from his jug and took a small swallow.

"How long?" she asked. "How long have you known me?"

"About six years. I saw you working with Mica, the group leader."

"And you never thought to talk to me?"

"No," he started. *'How do I say this?'* then said "You were too beautiful. You could have any man you wanted. My friends said you were of very high rank."

"Ah," she said and took another swallow. *'That explains his reluctance.'*

She watched him take a sip, hardly a swallow.

"So you chose to be friends with …other women?"

'Uh, oh…' he thought. *'Time to be careful.'*

"Not so much chose, as they chose me."

"Chose you?" She wanted to say *'How?'* and took another swallow of *ale*.

"The priests say if you put a flower in front of a honey bee the bee will know the flower."

"So you *knew* these women who wanted you?"

"You have turned my words against me," he remarked and raised his jug. He looked at the jug briefly. An image of a rabbit caught in a snare flashed through his mind. *'Do I want to be caught?'* he pondered.

She watched him swallow. He lowered his jug. "They both had red hair?"

"They did?" She knew from 'red hair' that they were not 'helpless' Beag women. She knew they were of Aryan descent, possibly from the northern lands.

She took a swallow, raised the jug to look inside. An eyebrow raised, she said "Empty."

Deem brought out the third jug and using his teeth pried out the stopper. He kissed the top rim of the jug and said, "From my lips to yours."

"You should be whipped for your superior attitude." She took the jug and looking into his eyes said, "You asked."

"What did I ask?"

"If we could be friends." She felt brave. The *ale* made her bold.

Deem took the stopper he held and jammed it into his jug. He put the jug on the ground and looked around. He was suddenly aware of his surroundings. They were in shadow. The sun was behind the mountains to the west. In the far distance he saw heat shimmering off the White Sea. High above, in light clouds he heard the call of a hawk calling her mate. He looked toward the washing house and saw two women looking in their direction. He saw the one they call 'Seth' up on a roof, doing guard duty in the early evening.

"What is your answer?"

He took her jug from her hand and raised it to his lips for a sip. When he returned it to her hand she said "We are friends" and took a big swallow from the jug.

He nodded and moved a little closer to her until his hip touched hers. She did not complain. She looked up at the hawk and began to stand but wobbled and put her hand on his knee as she sat down.

"My, this is good."

"We are friends," he said.

She turned to look in his direction. She did not look at his face. "I like you?" she said quietly almost as if she was not quite positive about her feelings.

She raised her jug and took another swallow. One eyebrow went up. She waited.

"Yes, we are friends," he said as if he did not believe it.

"That is not what I asked."

She waited. She saw his face wrinkled in a frown, then his face relaxed and he said, "Yes, I honor the lady."

She reached over and smacked his leg hard and looked him in the eye.

Deem laughed. "You persuade me," he remarked, and added "I like you."

At this admission she smiled and raised her hand to touch his face. "I feel generous."

"My lady?"

"Is there any gift I can grant to you?" She raised her jug and swallowed.

"No, my lady." He mumbled and added "I serve my lady."

She raised an eyebrow and smiled and placed her hand on his shoulder.

"I can think of something…" she began then stopped. She watched him take a swallow from his jug and then she did the same. "But not tonight."

She began to stand, felt dizzy and swung her jug so it hit him in the stomach. He bent over slightly but placed it on the bench. She leaned in one direction then back and said, "I need your help."

He stood and put his arm around her. "We walk."

She took a step and her leg buckled. He braced her and pulled her up.

Slowly, they took a step followed by another step. He looked up and realized the grove was dark. No one could see them.

Celi looked up at him with a grin and said, "Yes, you know, I like you."

"And I like you."

She stopped. He could see she was confused.

"We must keep moving. It is time to get you to your temple."

"And my sleeping platform," she added.

"Well, that would be a gift."

"What gift?" she mumbled.

"Your…" he began. After a moment of clear thought, he said "No."

"Yes, I think." She shook her head to clear it.

He walked with her, supported her all the way to the door to her temple. At the door they were met by Sara who tried to help Celi but Celi pushed her away.

"I want my friend to help me. He knows to where I am …where I want?"

She seemed to regain her sense of where she was and took his hand and pulled him through the main hall into the back rooms. When they reached her sleeping room she said, "Close the door."

He did. When he turned around she stood with her back to him and her arms straight out. "I like you and I know what I want."

He paused. He did not know how he came to be here.

"Take my robe off me," she laughed. "You know how, I believe."

"My lady?"

"Do you like me? Now. I know what I want."

"Yes, I like you, but…"

At that point Deem decided to act on his impulse. He put his arms around her middle. She did not protest. She placed a hand over his hand and raised it to her breast.

"Are you sure, my lady?"

She laughed quietly and said, "I know what I want."

Chapter 22

When the Lady Celi walked out to the fields in the morning, she usually wore a pair of light colored trousers under a tunic of white cloth. Someone gave her a hat of straw in a cone shape that she tied under her chin.

In the morning after Deem returned the two 'partners' walked out to the fields with empty sacks and digging sticks. They were determined to add to the harvest of radishes from their fields. Deem wore nothing on his head; on his hip a leather pouch hid a 'shooter' that fired a lead pellet. When Celi asked, he said,

"Not accurate, except at close range."

"Not what, but why do you wear it?" she asked.

"You are a princess."

"I do not feel like royalty. My head hurts this morning. You are afraid of me, is that why you wear that weapon?"

"You are the royal, descended from who? Some old guy?"

She began to laugh at his disrespect. She put her hand under his arm when she stepped over two rows of radishes and nodded toward the area they were going to pick. Some of the women working with Eglan were farther out in the field.

"You have rank. You are entitled to a guard."

"That is why I waved off your guard," he added. Deem reached over to put her hand on his arm just as they reached a white stake in the row.

"Right here," she said. "Eglan marked the row for us."

Deem looked at his stick. It was a short piece of tree branch with a smaller 'limb' cut to form a 'V' used for digging. He knew how to use it. She chuckled to herself and said in a low voice, "Can the mighty Pilot work in a field?"

"I imagine I can, if you can."

"But I had more practice back in Eridu. You were always off somewhere, fishing or chasing creatures in the forest."

"Is that how you think of me?"

"Ah, my love," she began and stopped.

'My love?' he thought.

A man she did not recognize was approaching the field from the direction of the Great Lake. His face was haggard; his hair dirty and snarled. He carried a sack over his shoulder; his feet were covered with mud. When he reached the radishes he walked down the row, which brought him toward Celi and Deem.

The man was 20 paces from Celi when Deem raised a hand to stop. The man took two more steps then stopped. He looked at the two of them then bowed, and said, "Can you tell me where to find Eglan?"

"We might," said Deem.

He looked the man up and down and said, "Who are you?"

The man made a small bow toward Deem, then said, "And just who do you think you are?"

"I am Deem, pilot of the *Dara* which you see over by that large building with the two smoke towers. I am partner to the Lady Celi."

"Well," said the man. "You are certainly full of yourself, just like my officer in the Army of Enlil, as it is called."

"Who are you?" he paused, "...before I lose my patience with you?"

"Well, my lord, I am Ashur, 'partner' as you say it to Eglan, my beloved mate."

"How do we know this?" said Celi.

"The woman speaks," said the man Ashur, incredulous.

"Chew your lips," said Deem using an expression old by many generations when his ancestors lived in the dry lands to the far west.

"The woman is Celi," she began, "the woman of rank who will have you whipped for your impertinence."

Ashur stood and looked at her, then at Deem. "As you say."

Then he bowed slightly and added, "I stand in your shadow, my Lady." This was an old expression used in the Land of the Pyramids. "And to you, Pilot Deem."

The man put his sack on the ground. He stepped into the next row of radishes and stretched his back. "I paid a man to deliver me. He put on a load of salt in Sodom and when I awoke the next morning, he was gone."

"Gone to where?"

"Back to Enlil's Army.

"How do you come to leave the Army?"

"We received a message. My beloved is with child."

"She is?" stammered Celi.

Deem turned to her with a raised eyebrow. "I did not know," said Celi while she pushed her straw hat away from her face. She turned and pointed to where Eglan worked with six other women.

They watched the man walk toward Eglan and the women who were digging the 'unholy' weeds. Deem glanced at Celi then back at the workers in the distance. Without looking he said, "You said, *'My love'* to me."

"Yes."

"Can you say it one more time?"

"Yes, I can."

"Well?"

"And what shall I receive?" she asked in the voice of a little girl about to receive a gift from her father.

"What do you wish to receive?"

"You, my love."

Deem turned to look into her eyes. "Your words say much."

Celi raised her hands to his face and cupped his cheeks. She leaned into him and kissed his nose.

Deem looked quickly in the direction of the field workers but no one was watching the two of them. He paused and put his hands on her shoulders and said, "And you, my love."

Celi turned her face down. When she looked up at him there was a drop of wetness in the corner of her eye.

"There is pain in my heart," he added.

"Yes. Will it always be this way? You are here when the sun goes down behind the mountains and then you leave after the sun rises in the east?"

"My love …there I said it again," and he added, "I may have to choose between my role as pilot and my love for you at this moment."

"Between *Dara* and me, a lowly female with her feet in the dirt?"

"Yes, that will be the dilemma." He laughed, and clapped his hands together. "There will be a dilemma. I will have to choose."

"Only if I agree to be your mate." Celi said these words. She felt a strange pain in her chest. She could not know if he was the one to whom she should be mated. And she remembered her Misha saying, 'Beware of men. They desire women for a short time.'

When Celi asked why a short time Misha warned her that men lose interest. That was the day Misha told her granddaughter about her first mate the one who took an interest in another woman, left with a hunting party and never returned.

Celi looked at Deem and said nothing. She lowered her face again.

"I envy that man and his Eglan. And Harn and his mate Gran. I hear she also is with child."

"It is the planet," she answered with a laugh. "Being on your back to make a baby must work."

He looked at her. Something said, 'Stay' but he felt a pull to get moving in *Dara.* He leaned forward and kissed her on the forehead. She looked up at him and said, "So, go!" To Celi, 'Go' felt like a swear word.

After Deem left her friend Gran walked out to where she tried to work but kept thinking about his behavior. Gran walked over to her and said, "He gave me his digging stick."

"He had to leave," mumbled Celi.

"You were seen with him in the grove."

"Yes. One thing led to another."

"What do you mean?"

"I think I should feel regret. But I do not."

"Regret about what?"

"His behavior. He took advantage of me..." she started then quickly stopped. She knew Gran was her oldest friend, but how much should one share?

"He is always *leaving*," she said and said no more while she worked.

Chapter 23

That evening Eglan brought one of her field workers to Celi with a complaint. The woman, said Eglan, was complaining about back pain while she worked and two of her friends reported she had been sick several times in early morning. Her friends probably wanted to make conditions better for their friend.

Eglan reported that she believed the woman had slept with one of the guards. Harn, standing in back of the room in the 'temple' added, "No, none of my guards."

When Celi said, 'How do you know?' the director of the guards said, 'well, I asked them,' to which several of the women present laughed.

Celi looked at the woman Nanar. "Can you continue to work in the fields?"

The woman probably thought she was being offered a reprieve and said, "No, my lady, the bending gets my back to making twinges."

"Are you weak in the morning?"

"I get confused and walk in the wrong places."

Someone in the group standing behind the woman said, "She gets confused easily and sleeps with the wrong man." There was more laughter.

Nanar's head jerked around with fire in her eyes.

"Is that true?" said Celi. She stared at the woman.

The woman said nothing. Celi repeated herself.

The woman said, "Do not be harsh, my lady."

"Is that true?" said Celi for the third time.

"Yes."

"Do you remember the punishment?"

"He was not my mate. I have no mate"

"Did he have a mate?"

"I did not enjoy his attention. When I said, No! ...he ignored me."

Celi considered this situation, and asked again: "Did he have a mate? It was a man was it not? From this village of Arad?"

"Yes, my lady, from this village. He has a mate."

"Will you tell us his name?"

The woman stood quietly and looked at Celi then around at the group in the room. Her eyes did not stop on anyone. The person she sought was not present.

"My lady," said Eglan. She was nominally in charge of the field workers.

Celi said "Do you know the punishment"

To which Eglan replied, "I do."

"How should I rule?" asked Celi. As in any army the field hands had a person, Eglan, who gave them directions. Her opinion carried weight with Celi's decision.

Eglan thought for a moment then lowered her head and without looking at Nanar said, "We all know the penalty is death."

The group of women, with the guards standing outside their circle, became quiet and looked at Lady Celi. Someone quietly said, "Mercy."

"There is a problem, here. I do not know the name of the man." She told Nanar to stand directly in front of her where she could see her eyes.

"You will tell us his name," She said in harsh sounds.

"No, my Lady. He is the father of my…"

"That is what Eglan and I think. He will be a father." She looked across the small gathering of women and then paused.

"Well, we have a dilemma." Someone in the crowd said, "Mercy." Celi looked at the gathered women and said, "Here is my decision."

"You will be sentenced to two years in our other post, the cave up the valley. For now, Gran will go with you." When she looked at Gran she saw only despair. "Harn and two men will haul bedding and cooking pots and storage pots of our crops up to the cave. You will begin to make the cave useable."

From the back of the group Harn said, "What of the large cat?"

"The cat will decide if Nanar should live. She will deal with the cat before Gran is permitted to enter."

They set out in the morning with one wagon loaded with supplies for the cave. Their task was to reach the base of the path that led upward. Harn, his mate Gran, another guard Seth and the woman Nanar left with the large water jugs and a few pots and blankets. The two men walked until they reached steeper hills then all four walked.

The sun moved in the sky. The vertical valley ahead loomed over them. In mid-afternoon they neared the mouth of the valley. Scattered green trees stood on precarious perches on the rocky slopes above the path. There were large rocks and the occasional falling stone. The stream from above moved quickly past the narrow opening as it fell gradually toward the village of Arad.

In late afternoon there were deep shadows in the valley. Sun bathed the brown and black rocks in the higher cliffs. When they reached the canyon mouth they stopped. Seth took the two horses to the river to drink. Later he hobbled them near an old gnarled tree. Harn gave the women the lighter loads of bedding to take to the cave. Then he realized they could not make it before nightfall and they camped near the wagon.

"What did my Lady mean 'to deal' with the cat?" asked Nanar.

"You will deal with the cat," remarked Gran.

"How?"

"I will give you a spear. You can drive it out of the cave."

Harn looked at her then added, "Be strong. It is possible the cat has already left for higher places in the mountains."

He looked at Gran who added, "I believe the Lady knew the cat may have moved."

"Your words, they mean ..."

"You had to be punished. Lady Celi could not punish your child could she?"

Chapter 24

In the late afternoon, two days after Harn and his companions left, Eglan brought a new complaint to Lady Celi. From what she could see, Sinar, the mate of Char, was showing bruises on her arms. That morning Eglan saw her cringe when a woman touched Sinar's side under her arm. When Eglan asked Sinar how she felt, the woman said nothing. One of her work mates noted that Sinar had been sleeping with her mate for the last ten days.

A second woman said she heard loud voices and what sounded like a person being struck with a hand.

Eglan and Celi chose to talk to Sinar's mate Char privately. When they talked to him, he said she had fallen down, and added that she was clumsy. When Eglan pressed him to explain, he began to say,

"She was hurt when she was with…"

Char stopped and stood quietly. He looked around, as if looking for a way out of the large room in 'Celi's' temple.

"With who?" demanded Celi.

The man stood silent. He looked at Celi briefly, then at Eglan. Then he began a long dialog:

"A man is allowed to dream, is he not? To dream of one day holding his son? To dream that one day his son will join his father in working together? I have that right, do I not?"

"That may be true," said Celi. She looked up when the old woman who cooks for her appeared at the door. She waved her away.

"That may be true," repeated Celi.

"What of it?" added Eglan.

"It is my right," said Char. He stood a little taller. "So, when my friend asked if I would share Sinar with him, I asked for a large bag of dates that he brought from Sodom. He agreed."

"For what purpose?"

"A double purpose," said Char. "The man has two sons already. I knew he could provide me with a son. And I could travel to Salem with a load of onions and trade the dates for a weapon to protect our village."

"Is it your role to acquire weapons?" asked Eglan.

"No, mistress." Char stood and stared at Celi. He did not look down and his face began to show color. Then he added, "My mate Sinar does as I tell her. I ordered her to sleep with the man."

"His name is..." began Celi.

"I do not chose to..." he began before Celi added, "You will be whipped. Ten strokes in front of the women. And the other man will receive twenty strokes before he is hung. If you do not name him, you will receive his twenty strokes on top of your ten strokes and the women in this village shall enjoy watching you hang."

Char began to sink as if his knees were weak. Then he straightened while the meaning of her words sank in. "I am stronger than you are, Lady See-Leest-Ay," he said with a snarl.

"The whipping shall be carried out in the morning." She stopped and looked at Char.

"He is gone. He lives in Sodom."

"You will have ten days to recover from the whipping then you and Harn and four others shall go to Sodom and bring the man back to me."

When Char said nothing, she added, "If you fail, you will suffer the fate that I have decreed for the other man."

Eglan mentioned the matter of Nanar and the un-named man. Celi looked at her as if she was puzzled, then added,

"If I find out you are the man who spent time with Nanar..."

"You will do what?" asked Char quickly.

From the back of the large room, near an opening, came the voice of Deem. He was dressed in his red tunic with his black hat. He wore a belt that held the leather pouch with his 'shooter' on his hip. "You will show respect to the Lady," he said when he began to cross the room.

Char began to back away from Celi and Eglan, moving in the direction of the far opening to the outside. He said nothing.

"You are too merciful," said Deem.

Celi looked up at the tall man with the straight nose and smiled. She shook her head. "He knows what will happen."

"If you be lenient," added Deem, "they will come to know you are weak. They begin to disrespect you."

"I showed mercy where it was necessary, with Nanar who is sentenced to two years' service in the mountains."

"And with Char?"

"The whip for abusing his mate. The other man will hang."

She said no more. She could not hang Char. It was the other man who violated the law against 'knowing' a woman who was not his mate. Celi looked up at Deem and smiled. He made a small bow to her and Eglan bowed and left. A small breeze entered the cavernous room and ruffled the wall hangings.

There were six chairs made of roughly hewn lumber with leather to fit the user's backside. Deem walked to one and plopped into the chair.

Celi walked over and looked down at him. He was her friend but there were times when she felt he was a stranger. It had been ten days since his last visit; ten days was a long time when you have strong feelings for your mate.

"You abuse your privilege, Pilot Deem."

"How?" he replied.

"You sat in the presence of your Lady without my permission."

"Ah," he said slowly. He smiled up at her and began to rise but she put her hand on his shoulder and pushed him back down.

"Will you threaten me with the lash? Again?"

"I think not," she laughed.

Celi smiled. She liked the way he answered her complaints. *'He is such a rogue,'* she thought, *'that I cannot help but like him after what we have together.'*

"What do you hear of the anger of Enlil toward the son of Enki, this one called Mar.Duk?"

He looked at her and began to slowly pull himself out of the chair. "My friend Seth and his mate have been slowly reading a tablet. The tablet says Enlil and Enki are half-brothers. Their two sons want to rule the four regions. That is the source of the conflict. Mar.Duk was the power behind the battles with the four Kings, some years ago." [End Note 16]

"So he wants more power?"

"Sand builds hills," added Deem.

"So he has the sand?"

"What he does not have is Enlil's control of Tilmun."

Celi turned away and walked to the entry doors of 'her' temple. She pushed one door open and stood to look out over the valley. *'How bad will it be?'*

She sensed more than heard Deem coming up behind her. He placed his hands on her waist and was about to lean down toward her neck when she said, "Gran and Sara are coming."

Celi twisted out of his grasp and queried… "What are you not telling me?"

Deem saw the two women coming from the cooking house and took a step back from Celi. "I will tell you later. I am heading for the washing house."

"Is this how you disrespect a lady who asks a question?"

"It is only because I respect you," he said and added, "that I will be presentable when I make my *'report'* to the Lady Celi."

He turned and walked backward away from her. As Gran and Sara came past him he made an exaggerated bow toward Celi and said, "Thank *you* my Lady." She smiled and her tongue caressed her lips.

Chapter 25

The first thing Deem revealed to Celi when he returned from *Dara* wearing a clean uniform was news about troop movements in Shin'ar, the valley between the two rivers.

"Mar.Duk's army is moving. It is in the mountains east of the White Sea."

Celi was seated at the small table in her sleeping room that she used for preparing her face. Her maid Sara was cutting her hair to a length the women called 'second knuckle,' the length of the two joints in her first finger. Celi had spoken publicly about short hair being easier to wash, even though the opportunities to wash hair were rare.

She reached up and ran her hand through her short hair. She was satisfied and told Sara to bring a jug of the herbal drink from the cooking house.

When she stood the soft white robe she wore reached to her ankles. Celi placed a wide cloth belt around her waist and tightened it. She walked to the two chairs with the leather backing and nodded to them. They both sat. He smiled at her.

"I knew what you just told me."

"Gran has been telling me about the Great Flood."

"What was this flood?"

"It was a mass of water hundreds of feet deep; it covered the earth."

"All the earth?"

"Except the mountain tops."

"How did that happen?"

"A planet passed by. The Lords knew it was coming. Lord Enlil decided to punish the children of Earth, the *children* of the Watchers who came down to mate with Daughters of Earth. The Watchers were evacuated. They saw the death of their children from the heavens; there was much turmoil and weeping." [End Note 17]

Celi was quiet. She used a short brush to clean her scalp. She turned toward Deem with a look of distress on her face.

Deem turned away. He looked at Sara who was using a small brush to sweep the deck of Lady Celi's room. "Should this maid be here?"

The maid Sara straightened up and said, "As my mistress wishes," and bowed toward Deem.

To the maid he said, "Go and ask the cook for her best herbal drink, cold, three of her baked rolls and meat with onions. We will eat here," added Deem.

"Go and find Gran. Send her to me," said Celi.

As Sara left Celi said, "She is learning."

"I almost trust her as I do not trust most of '*my*' women."

He watched the maid leave.

On the path up to the cave, Nanar carried an old spear given her by Harn. It was a sturdy pole onto which a sharp spike of forged iron had been grafted. She had pulled her long hair back and wrapped it. Harn allowed her to wear both of her coats as extra protection. She felt her legs were exposed; she thought the cat might attack her legs.

The air was brisk; the day was clear as she walked slowly up the path. The heat of the sun felt good in her hair. She was about to turn a corner around a large boulder when a ground bird, large enough to eat, suddenly jumped into her path. Nanar reacted on instinct; she threw her spear.

Her spear bounced off a stone in the path. The tip came up and struck the bird in the neck. Nanar ran forward; the bird struggled. She put the spear across the bird's neck. With her foot on the spear she reached down and broke the bird's neck. Coming around the rock behind her, Harn said,

"What will you do with that thing?"

Nanar looked at the limp bird for a long time. Then she smiled. She asked Harn for his cutting knife and began to cut the bird into pieces. She threw the feathers over the edge of the path.

"Throw a piece into the cave. Wait a while. Throw a piece into the cave mouth and outside the cave. If the cat comes out I will prod it to move into these mountains," she said proudly.

The ten days Char was allowed to recover from his whipping passed quickly. On the tenth day Celi sent Char with Seth and two guards to Sodom. Five days later they walked into Arad, after a long trek to Sodom and back. Their faces were covered in dust; their hair matted; their clothes carried mud. Behind them came a stranger with a rope fastened around his neck. Seth pointed at the post in the center of the plaza in front of Celi's Temple. Char and the guards tied the man with each arm on one side of the post. They ran a rope through an iron ring and pulled his arms up until he stood on his toes.

Seth pointed at two of the guards and they took up station at opposite sides of the post, their backs to the prisoner.

Seth brought a cloth bag over to Char and opened it. He gave a jug to Char who took it to one of the guards. The guard sniffed the jug and took a long swallow. Char took the jug to the second guard and he also took a long swallow.

Char gave the jug to Seth who also sniffed the contents. "Five days older, would you say?"

"Aye, we have earned this drink," said Char.

Seth raised the jug, took a drink and spent some time considering the contents. He swallowed and snorted, "Whew, you are correct."

One of the maids who serve Lady Celi walked up to Char and said, "My mistress wishes you to visit the Washing House then she will meet you and Seth here at the post."

Chapter 26

"Your name is?" said Celi to the man tied to the post. The sun was touching the mountains when Celi and two male guards stepped out of her temple. She wore a black gown to signify her intent to administer the law; over her head she placed a black cloth that partially hid her face.

"Water."

Celi looked at Seth then at Char. "How long with no water?"

"Two days," said Char.

She looked at Harn then at the small crowd that was growing on the plaza. She looked down at her emblem of office, the silver ankh from Lady Ninki, and said, "No water?"

"My lady," began Char, hoping to please her. "He comes to be punished. He deserves his thirst."

"So he does."

She looked at the jug in Char's hand and pointed at the prisoner. Char opened his mouth to protest and stopped. Celi pointed at the prisoner. Seth said, "That was to be Char's reward for the long trek yesterday and today."

"Char does not deserve a reward."

"Yes, my lady," said Char quickly. He held the jug where the prisoner could drink from the open mouth of the jug. He watched as the man drank until the jug was empty, and Char backed away from the man.

"What is your name? The Lady Celi demands you answer."

The man said nothing. He leaned in and wiped his chin on the post. Celi saw his silence, shook her head and said "Apply the whip."

Char unhooked his whip from his belt and snapped it back toward the witnesses. He flicked it forward to gauge the distance. "I am ready," he said in a soft voice.

"You will tell us your name," said Celi. She nodded at Char and the whip flew smartly across the plaza before it bit into his back. She nodded again and Char applied the whip. The man jumped a little, as if stung by a scorpion. She nodded again and again the whip attacked the man's back.

"Malor," said the man.

Celi held up a hand to stop Char and his whip. "So tell me, Malor, how many dates did you pay to Char?"

"A large bag of dates," he said. "I could barely lift it."

"Did you hit Char's mate, Sinar?"

"It was an accident," he said with strong conviction. Celi nodded at Char and once more the whip bit into Malor's back.

"Stop, I ask you ...my lady?"

Celi held up a hand to stop Char. "We stop," she said then added in a soft voice, a voice to convey hope, "Tell me the truth now, did you sleep with Sinar?"

"Sleep? No, mistress. She would not let me sleep," he made a guttural sound. "She kept pestering me for, you know, more of me and then she climbed on top and really seemed to enjoy herself."

"Do you know the penalty?"

"I buy what I get," said Malor. "I always pay."

"In this case, you have bought yourself a rope."

The man looked at Celi for a long moment while he absorbed her words. "Can there be mercy?"

"No, you have convicted yourself out of your own words." She turned her back to the man and walked to Char. She pointed at the Temple where an arch formed the entry. "You see the iron ring above the entry?"

Char nodded.

"Then hang this piece of Beag trash, slowly, after you cut off his male member as a warning to any man who might do likewise."

"Mistress, did you forget? I am Beag," said Char with anger in his voice.

"You caused this spectacle. You finish it." She walked into her temple to the farthest room. Time passed slowly. When it happened she almost did not hear the man's screams.

Chapter 27

The weather turned cool, briefly. The women working in the fields were given a day of rest. They received several jugs of the wicked concoction made by the guards, which the women called 'Bite of the Apple.' Celi walked out to the edge of the river and saw a quiet land. The fields were almost empty of workers. Two women were moving the tubes that brought water into the fields. To the north she saw *Dara* near the end of the old road. Two guards were standing near it. Movement near the Washing House caught her eye and she saw Deem and his Second, called Aonim, moving toward the Cooking House.

She was pleased with their progress. Seventeen of the houses now held flat roofs. None of the 30 women were sleeping under the stars. The men had their own 'camp' if that was the word in what had been a warehouse. The two women in charge of the Washing House were justifiably proud of the clean walls and floors of their facility. Celi had tried to convince them not to change the water in the washing pool each day, without results. One said she had a plan to bring water in a channel directly into her 'temple.'

Celi was equally pleased with the support they received from Captain Deem and the *Dara.* This day, when they arrived, they brought bags and bags of cucumbers, tomatoes, melons and apples. They also brought a flat box with dirt that held 30 sprigs of apple trees, to be planted.

She was walking past the Cooking House when the old cook came out and said, "Do not give that pilot a heaping of praise. The tomatoes he brought are old, some of the shells are cracked and the insides are shriveled."

"Thank you," she responded.

"The Lords," said Deem after they walked out to her grove. She had begun to think of it as her grove when the guards put up a frame and tent material over her bench. "The Lords," he said, "are making frantic plans to lift their children out of the areas where the two armies will someday face each other."

The morning was clear, even if it was crisp. Light clouds streamed across the sky. The mist rising from the White Sea suggested fog, an unheard of event. South of the White Sea they could just see smoke from cooking fires; the fore-runners of Mar.Duk's army had set up camp.

Celi wore her long white robe and sandals. Her hair was brushed and stood away from her scalp. Celi placed her hand on his knee and said, "We have people in the southern army."

"They are Beag, after all," he said and waved away a pesky insect.

She was silent and watched distant clouds climb over the southern mountains. She knew Enlil's Army was beyond those mountains. "We must warn them."

"Warn them?" he mused. "You do not trust them."

"We must try. Their mates are here in my village."

"And you *must?*" he asked.

"I am Celi. I *must.*"

He looked at her hand on his knee. He was quiet. "Have you forgiven me?"

"For?"

"For what happened in your sleeping room?"

"I like you, but how do I forgive you?"

"You take my hand and tell me we are still friends."

"Friends?" she frowned. "We are more than friends."

"What then?" His eyebrows formed a question.

Celi turned to look at him and added, "I say 'I like you' but you do not respond."

Deem sat in a quandary. He knew what she wanted him to say but the words would not come. At the same time, he thought, *'I cannot say 'I love you.' I am not sure. What if she decides I am not worth a bag of onions?*

Instead he said, "How will you warn them?"

"Send someone."

"Do you care so much …they are…?"

"Mates to my women here at Arad."

"I will take your warning," he said while leaning to kiss her lips. She turned her face and he kissed her cheek briefly.

Chapter 28

"It is strange how these royals prepare for war," said Deem when he walked off the ramp at the rear of *Dara*. The day was almost over; the sun was behind the mountains to the west.

"Five days this time," said Celi in a quiet voice. She stood next to him, head bowed. She had walked in from field work in the onion fields.

Deem smiled and said, "Yes, my love."

She knew he did not mean *'my love.'* He was dirty after five days of almost constant flight and needed to visit the Washing House.

He turned and saw Celi in her white work clothes, with dirt in the knees of her trousers. When she removed her conical hat he reached up and plucked an onion stem from her short hair. There was a smudge of dirt near her nose; freckles were scattered under her eyes. She licked her lips; he thought about kissing her. Standing here outside 'her' village in full view of her women field workers, he decided to avoid the trouble such an action might cause.

"You said it was strange?"

"Yes, they build trenches around Salem."

"That is north from here."

"They are being careful, I guess."

"We brought children from Ur and Nippur to Salem. Their mother, Princess Inanna thanked me with a basket of fruit."

"There must be a reason," she said. *'Who is this princess?'*

"There must be," he responded, and thought, *'the Princess tells me there are storm clouds on the horizon. Such an unusual expression.'*

"Is she easy to look at, this Princess Inanna?"

"Her beauty exceeds all the deep red color of the sky just before the Sun falls off the earth." Deem smiled to himself. Then he realized what he just said to Celi.

"She is beautiful, then?" End Note 18

Deem put his hands on her shoulders and said, slowly, "Her beauty is but a dim reflection of *your* beauty. You are more beautiful than the red turning into pale red just before the sun revisits the earth. Your beauty out-shines the light blue of our pale sky in early morning."

Celi's lips formed into slight smiles. One eyebrow went up as if to ask, *'Who told you to flatter your me?'*

Deem reached into his bag of equipment and produced a gift made of papyrus. The sheet was folded over itself into a square. A wax mass over the center of the square held the symbol of Lady Ninki. He held it out to Celi and said, "This came to me from Lady Inanna. She made me promise to put it into your hands."

Celi looked at the folded document and her face betrayed her sense of concern. She knew what this message might be.

"Make yourself presentable. We will open this together with Gran and Harn in my Temple."

She saw Eglan among the women and waved her over. Celi told Eglan to bring Harn to her Temple room after 'Lord Deem' was presentable.

She said this laughing with a hand open, as if 'presenting' Lord Deem.

His face was blank before he also began to laugh. "Are you presentable?" he quipped as he began to walk toward the Washing House.

Chapter 29

The Central Room of the Temple began to acquire a mystique, as if the people who lived in Arad knew the Temple held sacred mysteries. When Celi, Deem, Harn and Eglan gathered they stood near the new stone altar in the center of the meeting room. The walls had acquired large banners, made by two women using old blankets brought from Salem. One of the banners depicted Celi arriving; the *Dara* sat in the background. Deem, when he saw it, politely teased Celi. He laughed and said, "Where am I in this banner?"

She laughed and smiled, "Are you the goddess of this small village, this Arad?"

The altar was behind a sunken fire pit where coals heated and burned herbs. If the priestess (Celi) wanted the community to arrive, she would add chemicals that made the smoke white. There were six chairs in a circle around the sunken fire pit. The four friends, however, stood.

"We sent three wagons of food and three more large containers for water up to the cave. Four of the women have worked hard to get those supplies up to the cave," added Harn.

"She was brave, that Nanar." Harn scratched his hair above his ear. "She says the 'ferocious' cat swung his vicious claws at her and she thrust her spear."

"Are her words true?"

"Let's say they are. I was far back but I saw her throw the spear. It hit the ground and whacked the cat in the rear. The cat ran up the path then stopped. Nanar stepped around the large boulder and shouted at the poor cat. It turned and walked away, as if to say, *I go, you did not make me.*"

"She and Gran have moved the food to the back of the cave," added Harn with a note of pride.

"You are missing Gran, are you?" asked Celi.

"Yesterday she wanted to know why so much for only two women?"

"A friend warned me," said Celi. She did not say that it was Lady Ninki, the aged and somewhat infirm mate of Lord Enki.

"Warned you?" said Eglan with a look of concern. Her hands went around her swollen belly. "My mate should know about this."

"He does not know?" said Deem with a wicked smile.

"You mean," began Eglan, "...about the baby?" She chuckled.

Celi told Deem that Gran's mate Ashur had been in Arad for the past thirty days. "Of course he knows," she laughed.

"About what?" added Harn. He was confused.

"The Lords Enlil and Mar.Duk are at war," said Celi. She raised the folded papyrus and held it for her friends to see. She placed it against the edge of the altar and cracked the seal. She unfolded the crinkly item and found two words inside ... 'Misha Leona.'

She showed it to Deem who passed it to Harn and Eglan.

"What does it mean?" asked Eglan.

"We must take all our women and move to the cave."

"Do we have time?" asked Eglan.

"Two days it takes," added Harn. "One day to the valley, one up to the cave."

"There is other news," said Deem. "I was not going to tell you this," he said to Celi. "I was afraid for you. I want you to come aboard *Dara.*"

She looked at him and said, "What news?"

"Those camps south of the White Sea. Lord Enlil has a weapon, the Shar-Graz that will totally obliterate those camps."

"Oh, this is..." began Celi. "I have no words."

"There is worse..." added Deem. "Today I flew over the White Sea. The camp is large; it encircles the south edge of Sodom."

"A terrible place," said Harn. He added, "Perhaps the troops are to punish the wicked men?"

"How do you mean?" asked Deem.

"You cannot see their depravity from the air. The men have a fondness for boys," responded Harn. His eyebrow went up in a look of chagrin.

Celi looked at Harn for a moment then added, with slow words, "Our friend Char in the south. I sent him to tell our men to resist the orders of their officers and find protection in the mountains."

"He did not listen," said Harn. "We have a message. He formed a troop out of '*his*' men and is leading them."

Celi blew air out of her cheeks. Eglan turned away and said something like 'hard to believe' but her friends knew she meant the opposite. Deem shook his head and walked around the altar to put his arms around Celi. She looked up at him.

"We are going to the cave."

"I know," he began. "While I was in the Washing House, Aonim brought a message. I am ordered to remove any royals from Tilmun, the landing site."

"When you are there can you persuade Char and his men?"

"To do what?" asked Deem without a smile.

"I do not know..." Celi looked at Harn, then Eglan, then back at Deem. "Perhaps to tell the Beag who trust him to take their camels and head for shelter in the mountains?"

"Can you trust Char?"

"My guess is no. If he betrays us Char may die."

Chapter 30

Arad stood in shadow. The village was quiet. One guard stood lonely vigil on the roof of a house. The women were at their meal. Smoke rose from the chimney of the Cooking House. The women were baking a stew from the last of the available meat. The village seemed to hold a quiet expectation for tomorrow's caravan to the mountain cave.

When they walked out to the grove of trees Celi did not expect to convince her 'friend' Deem to leave his role as pilot. Nor did Deem expect to convince Celi to abandon 'her' women workers. They found wood burning in the fire pit. They sat. Celi looked out across the valley. The shadows cast by the setting sun stretched across the river and beyond their fields of radishes and onions.

"My love," said Deem quietly.

He had grown to like their favorite spot: the bench in 'her grove' where a small fire pit had been built. They sat and stared into the flames.

"Such soft words." She stared at the flames. Someone had brought an offering of old apple tree wood and left a pile of cut branches. Her nose liked the smell. There was so much she wanted to say, but could not. *There are other pilots who can fly Dara,* she thought sitting next to Deem. *Such as Aonim; you trained him well.*

"Come with us in the morning," she said and placed her hand on his knee.

He leaned back so he could see her face. He fumbled at his waist and managed to untie the belt that held his 'Shooter,' the small pistol. "I want you to have this."

"Should I wear it?" she began and added, "My love?"

"Wear my 'Shooter.' It gives you authority."

"Come with us," she said again.

"No, you are coming with me," he said slowly, barely hoping she would say 'Yes' but knowing she would stay with 'her' people.

She moved her hand up his back until she could pull him toward her mouth. She leaned up and into him and caught his lower lip between her teeth and said, "I am the Lady Celi, mistress of Arad."

He laughed.

"And I command you," she mumbled while her tongue explored his teeth. She withdrew her tongue and meshed her lips with his lips ever so softly and slowly. He hummed something, an old lover's tune.

"And now I command you to join me."

"Where would that be?"

She laughed. She took his hand and placed it on her leg. "Where we once joined each other."

"Ah," he mumbled and dropped his belt on the bench. "I must go in the morning."

"I must lead my people," she stated flatly.

She watched his reaction. He stood and offered her his hand. She added, "If I could I would go with you."

"I know," he said. His face had no expression.

"But for tonight," he began.

"I want to be under you." She softly caressed the muscles of his chest. He stood a little taller.

"And then the second time…"

"Second time?"

"I want to be on top." She took his hand and gently led him toward her 'Temple.'

Deem watched her as she led them around old stumps and through the young trees of the grove. Her face shone, as if she possessed some inner knowledge of the future. Or was it determination?

"I take it you want me to make an offering?"

She laughed.

"Yes, my love. A second time. It is time we make a baby."

An eyebrow went up in disbelief on Deem's face. Then he smiled.

It was only later that Celi realized she had offered and Deem had accepted. No questions, no promises. When she heard words about Deem and the temptress Inanna she began to wonder if she could hold onto her brave pilot.

Chapter 31

All four wagons were loaded. The four horses that belonged to Arad were about to haul their cargo up the long winding trail to the west, toward the path up the valley to the cave. Each wagon had been assigned six women who knew their task was to move the wagon if the horse faltered. They had thrown their bags of possessions onto 'their' wagons.

Three of the guards stood at the head of the caravan. One of them wore a rifle. They waited and watched the women prepare. The one called Ashur nodded toward Eglan and said, "My mate. Her stomach grows."

"We know," laughed Seth. "I saw Char smiling. He left ten days ago."

"He smiled?" said Seth.

"Yes. He smiled when he looked at your mate."

"My mate?

"Is there something she has not told you?" quipped Ashur.

Seth stood still while he looked down the line of wagons to where his mate was helping with a wagon. Then he looked up at Ashur and saw Ashur with a grin that could swallow an entire onion. He laughed.

"Perhaps we are better off that Char, his high holiness, has gone to join the army," laughed the third guard.

They watched Harn, their guard captain, as he stopped at each wagon to check on the women. When he reached the last wagon he talked to Celi. He waved an arm at the guards; his motion meant for them to begin. Seth turned to the nearest wagon and said, "We go."

One of the women took a long switch and snapped it on the rump of their horse. He turned to look at her as if to say, *'What?'* but took a first step forward and the wagon creaked. With his second step the wagon began to move. The six women walked beside the wagon. The guards turned and led the way.

At the rear of the caravan a load of onions, hidden under a mat of straw, waited for Lady Celi. Her badges of office were inside a small box at the bottom of the onions. It was hoped the straw would keep the onions cool. Celi and her maid spread blankets over the straw. The women of the wagon then placed their small bags over the blankets.

The second and third wagons began to move. On the third wagon she saw Mica. The women in his group made him ride their wagon. *That is right,* Celi thought. She saw her oldest maid Talinda coming out of the temple with a folded and wrapped package. Talinda presented the package to Celi.

"Your two red tunics and white trousers for the fields," she said.

"Have you considered your decision?"

"Yes, my lady. We stay. We were here when there was nobody. There are floors to wash; clothes to wash; we will enjoy the quiet.

"And your mate? Where is he?"

"He returns from hunting in two days, my lady."

"Very well, then."

Celi put the package with the other small bundles that nestled in the blankets above the onions. She saw they were being left behind and told Harn to get them moving. When the wagon began to move she turned to Talinda and said, "You and your daughter will be careful?"

"My mate, two days, the three of us will look after Arad."

Celi nodded her head. She thought of Deem and Aonim aboard *Dara* and the thirty Beag in the army with Char. She looked up the caravan with her own twenty-four brave women, a few with child, walking ahead of her. In her mind she saw the long path under a hot sun. She enjoyed the heat from the sun; her back felt relaxed. She remembered her grandfather Mica and his attention to the atmosphere and the vagaries of the winds. She remembered the feel of rain on her face the day she parted from Mica. *'What could I say about him?'*

'We will build a stela, here in Arad,' she thought. In her mind she saw her friends who might have been tortured or raped by Mar.Duk's men in Eridu.

She felt tired. This past night would be a memory she would hold and cherish. She tried to remember Deem's arms around her. She could taste his kisses on her lips, his kisses on her neck.

Talinda, who was standing nearby, suddenly said, "My Lady, your eyes?" then added, "Your eyes are leaking water."

Celi reached up and touched her eye. She brought her finger around to her nose and saw dampness, and smiled.

"It is good." She paused then added, "My grandmother always said 'There is no joy without first tears.'

"Yes, my Lady."

Celi watched Talinda walk toward 'her' Temple. She scanned the horizon and saw few clouds. She felt satisfied; they were prepared.

Chapter 32

At the end of a long day the caravan made camp at the opening into the mountains. They formed a square with the wagons and posted two guards outside the camp. Harn and Seth built a cooking fire in the center and the women boiled onions and some of their last supply of meat. It was tough meat, as some said, but they believed the boiling would make it tender.

"It was an old cow to begin with," said one of the women.

"Another of Char's foolish decisions," said another.

"We are not all foolish," said another referring to the women in their party. The wind from the valley became stronger just before a loud roaring was heard coming from the valley ahead of them.

The roaring became louder. Celi could feel the sudden increase in the wind coming out of the valley. "It's a blast of mashed air," she shouted at the women who were looking toward the valley.

The wind diminished during the night. By day break there was only a soft breeze flowing down through the rocky cliffs that guarded the valley and its canyon. The women boiled beans and onions for a meal and washed as they could in the swift stream that flowed out of the mountain gorge. Harn's men helped load bags of supplies onto the backs of the women. The group knew they faced an uphill climb with weight on their backs.

After the women left the men took the rifle and pointed it at the head of their oldest horse. The weapon banged, the horse dropped onto its side. Harn and his crew began to carve the horse. Lady Celi had asked, politely, that more meat be hauled to the cave.

Going up the path Seth took the lead, the women followed. The narrow path followed a mind of its own; it meandered up and around boulders then down and around other boulders. Always, the path rose upward. The sun was high over-head when the first of the long line reached the cave. They were welcomed by Gran and Nanar. Both women displayed enlarged breasts and long gowns tightly stretched across their bellies.

Gran was quickly told her mate Harn was coming up the path. Nanar showed Seth where to store his load of firewood while Gran led the women to the area for storing supplies. Six of the women were assigned to finish filling the large water jars. The long string of tired women brought their first loads into the cave. Celi arrived at the end of the 'walking caravan' as she described it.

After resting the women and the men who struggled up the path with loads of meat, already attracting black flies, turned to the path and walked down for a second trip.

They made the return trip up the path in less time. They carried smaller bags of supplies and their clothes. Harn brought an enormous pile of blankets up the path. Celi hauled a load of onions wrapped in one of her blankets. Two men came up the path slightly bowed from the weight of firewood on their backs.

The path was in shadow when the long 'caravan' reached the cave. Above them, the sun was beyond the mountain tops. A long shadow was cast across the flat land where stood Arad and across the eastern sea. In the far distance the shadow was beginning to paint darkness on distant mountain tops. Celi was at the end of the line, behind the men with the firewood. Directly ahead of her a flat boulder blocked the path.

A brilliant white flash lit the valley. The flash was intense; the stones and trees in the valley cast black shadows. Celi was frozen; she saw her shadow outlined on the flat granite rock. She began to turn to look toward the source; she stopped. The bright white light was beyond her experience; she felt humbled.

The light began to fade. Celi heard Harn call her name and she told him she was around the boulder. She turned toward the source and saw an enormous black cloud climbing into the red light from the setting sun. There were red flashes within the cloud; it grew and boiled into the heavens. She heard Harn approaching from behind.

"What is it?" he asked.

"I think I know," she began. "Deem warned me they might use the Shar.Graz, the weapon that is lifted into the sky on a blast of fire and falls onto an enemy. It is called the 'Brilliance of Enlil' for the whiteness of the light.

"Is that Sodom?"

"Yes."

As she said this a second white flash appeared. It was beyond Sodom in the area of two villages called Gomorrah and Zoar. A moment later the mountains to their south were back-lit by three white flashes that sent white light into the sky, illuminating high, thin clouds.

"Where is that?" asked Harn.

"The Land of Tilmun, the great southern peninsula, the restricted zone." She thought, *'An army moving south ...did they even have a chance against such a weapon?'*

"We should be inside the cave, mistress?"

"You go. I am behind you," she shouted. *"Time to walk,'* flashed through her brain. They began to move quickly toward the cave. The men with the firewood were entering the cave when an enormous 'Boom!' thundered up the canyon past their cave. Celi found herself at the entrance of the cave and saw a woman below her, lugging a water jar up from the stream below the cave. She shouted at her to hurry.

Standing there, at this elevated site, she realized the valley opened to the east, as if she stood at the head of a funnel. If wind came from the east, it would be compressed by the walls of the canyon. She looked down the canyon and saw a wall of black boiling and roiling from the direction of the eastern sea. She knew, without being told, that she must get out of the path of that cloud of death. She looked down at the woman with the water jar on her shoulder and shouted at her to drop it and run.

The woman looked up at her with confusion. This was the woman who spent her free time in Arad making pots and jars from river clay and tending them until the fire hardened them. The jar on her shoulder was probably one of her creations.

Celi saw the top of the black cloud, where it was illuminated by the setting sun, approaching the opening to the valley. She shouted once more but the woman continued to climb at a steady pace. Celi turned her back to the cloud and rushed into the cave. She shouted at her people to get down.

An enormous rush of air passed the cave entrance. Some of the air suddenly increased the air pressure on everyone's ears. Then the sound of small rocks thrown against the canyon walls made a rippling sound in the canyon. The air pressure diminished and the blast of air passed up the canyon.

Celi climbed to her feet and walked to the cave opening. There was no sign of the woman with the water jar.

Chapter 33

"Lady Celi, what must we do?" asked Gran.

"Stay in the cave until this black air has passed."

Celi turned to see most of the women in the cave were looking at her. They believed she must know the answers. Celi nodded at Harn and took him aside.

"We have water for four days. No one leaves the cave for four days," she said and added, "Post a guard. No one leaves."

To the women she explained that the black air outside was dangerous. They were to stay in the cave for four days and in the canyon for five days total.

Harn and two of the guards built a fire just inside the cave mouth. The fire was in the fire-pit Gran used for cooking. One guard was assigned to stand just inside the cave mouth and to feed the fire during the night.

Toward morning, when the eastern sky was barely pink, the guard heard a 'swish' overhead and looked up. He saw a flash of silver, possibly reflected from *Dara* when it turned to circle overhead. *Dara* did not land; it climbed into the sky and flew east over the black cloud.

In the early morning, the wind changed direction. A strong current came out of the mountains and down the canyon. It was a scrubbing wind. It scrubbed the canyon and its rocks and sent a blast of air through the canyon mouth. Beyond the canyon the air cleared and it appeared the lingering black cloud was moving off to the east.

Later that morning Harn told Celi that he could see their village Arad from the edge of the path. There was no apparent movement in the village, but then the distance was too great to see any details.

In late afternoon, before the sun touched the mountain tops 'behind' her canyon, Celi walked out quickly and looked to the east. She saw the black cloud was climbing up the mountains beyond the White Sea.

When she returned to the cave she told the women the black cloud had gone to the east. She then turned to Harn and asked what was beyond the mountains.

Harn was puzzled. He thought for a long moment. He looked at his mistress with confusion. He was not sure of her intentions in asking what was beyond the mountains to the east.

"Your city, Eridu and Ur and Lagash," he said. "And Babylon."

Chapter 34

"One of the women heard a whistle sound when the blast of heavy air went up the canyon," reported Harn.

Celi waited. She wore a puzzled expression.

"Farther back in the cave," he added.

Melan walked up and added, "I told Mica there may be an updraft."

She wore an old dress this day, instead of work trousers and a light caftan. The women knew they would not dig onions and radishes this day. Melan took pride in her appearance; her hair was braided and coiled around her head. She saw Celi looking at her head and added, "We could not sleep. We worked on our hair."

"The updraft?"

"Mica used an old hammer. There was a hollow sound. He hit the rock a mighty blow," added Harn, smiling. He was impressed with Mica's skill.

"And?"

"A piece of rock hit his shoulder. Mica is 'damaged' shall we say?"

"Not that badly," added Harn. "We will thank Mica."

"And?"

"We have an updraft. We will move the cooking fire into the cave."

"Thank you," said Celi without smiling. She went to Mica and gave him a hug. He was cheerful; said he saw the crack in the rock. Later that day she took Harn aside. Her message was simple: *We cannot afford to lose any of these women or the men. We have an old village to re-build.*

In the east, beyond the White Sea, the mountains on the horizon became visible near the end of the day. The ominous black cloud was gone, passed beyond the mountains. The sun shone down on Arad, the quiet town. The sun shone down on the camp site used by the women when they evacuated Arad. The entire valley, from west to east, was quiet. There were no birds, no animals.

The first blast of the 'Brilliance of Enlil' was south of the White Sea, the one they called *Yām-ha-Māret* (Sea of Death). The blast destroyed a once proud village. The walls of houses were crushed by a mighty weight. The defensive walls were pushed in by the force of the explosion. Their temple crumbled. The people who lived there with pride and contempt for the laws of Lord Enlil, the men who practiced an evil act with boys, all died. The village was quiet. The same fate was suffered by Gomorrah and Zoar.

A crack formed in the southern wall of the sea; water poured into the low lands beyond. The waters covered the ruins of the villages. The waters rose and rose until Gomorrah was seen no more.

The army had prepared to move. They were south of Sodom when the missile hit and obliterated the men, their wagons, their train of 'busy' women who follow an army always in search of work. Their hopes and fears for the future were wiped off the cosmic slate of the universe in one brash, ugly and painful moment under the white hot flash of Enlil's missile.

Chapter 35

"My mate Char?" said the woman. She wore her best dress and her short hair fell straight to her ears. Her face was the face of a Beag with a very slight brow-ridge above her eyes. She had the brown eyes and brown hair of a Beag; she was definitely not of Aryas stock. Her birth name La.Ra.Ak means 'brightening glow.' When Lara walked up to Celi and Harn, she bowed to both and made a slight smile. "I am here to ask about my mate."

"Your form is not correct," said Harn. "You should say *I ask the Lady Celi to favor my request for information."*

The woman stood taller for a moment. Her eyebrows formed into a frown. Then she bowed to Harn.

"Master Harn, I wish to ask..." she began.

"Yes, Lara, I understand," said Celi.

Celi reached over and patted Harn on the arm. "See to the cooking fire and ask the cooks to warm some herbals for Lara and Lady Celi."

Harn nodded and walked toward the fire where it burned inside the newly built fire pit. Celi took Lara by the arm and directed her toward planks that sat on top of empty storage boxes.

They sat and Celi said, "What of your mate?"

"What can you tell me?"

"You know I sent him to the army in the south?"

"Yes, he told me that much."

"It was punishment," added Celi quietly.

"I heard gossip from several of the women. They said nasty words to strike at me with their tongues and their vicious eyes."

"The ill wind blows from the east," noted Celi.

"One of our men said there was a flash?"

"The mountains were lit by three flashes."

"Were they like the one that brought the Black Cloud?"

"Yes," said Celi. '*This woman must know the truth, or should I help her hold onto vague hopes?'*

"Char was directed to find the thirty Beag men we sent down there to serve two years in the Army of Enlil in Tilmun, the land beyond those southern mountains."

"Yes?" said Lara. She watched while one of her friends brought two small bowls of hot herbal potion. She took her bowl and smelled the herbals and raised an eyebrow.

"Char was directed to take his men into the mountains for their safety." Celi watched while Lara took a tentative sip of the herbal.

"So he is alive then?"

"I want to say ...Yes."

"He was not a good man," said Lara. "He beat me."

"There were reports," said Celi.

"And he abused two of my friends."

"What are you telling me?"

"Of the three of us, we voted last night." Lara took another sip of the herbal and tasted her lip with her tongue trying to decipher the taste.

"You voted?"

"We voted. We do not care if he is alive. We prefer dead."

Celi saw Harn nearby and waved him to come over. "Take Lara to her sleeping station. She needs sleep."

When Lara began to ask, Lady Celi told her the herbal potion contained an elixir to help her sleep. Then Celi apologized. She feared Lara might be distraught if she knew her husband Char was dead. Lady Celi then moved to her sleeping pallet and placed her head on a rolled up blanket. The smell of onions was strong. She began to smile to herself and hoped the herbal was strong. Three days without sleep was one too many.

Chapter 36

Day five began with a bang, or a whimper depending on your perception of the tension in the cave. The rising sun was only a weak suggestion in the eastern sky when the groans of Eglan became louder. The entire cave knew she was about to present her mate with a baby.

The two women who were helping Eglan became frustrated with Ashur and told him to slice a pile of wood into shavings and be prepared to heat a blanket to receive his child.

After the sun cleared the mountains in the east, the women began to tell Eglan she should scream. They knew she was trying to keep her pain inside; she should let it out. Everyone in the cave knew she was trying to be brave. It was time to stop the groaning.

One of the women said, "Now!" forcefully. Eglan screamed with a force that knocked small dust mites off the roof of the cave. One of the women placed a white cloth under the head of the baby and helped it to depart from its mother.

She held the baby by its ankles and smacked it on the rump. The baby made an intake of breath then cried loudly in protest. In the momentary silence following the baby's scream, the people in the cave smiled at each other. The woman turned toward the cooking fire and told Ashur he was the father of a baby girl.

Mid-morning the sky was a brilliant blue color. There was a slight breeze from the west; a small bird came down the valley and found a site to build a nest inside the gnarled branches of a stubborn pine that refused to let go of its precarious perch on the rocky slope of the canyon.

Into this quiet scene came the sudden 'thunder' of the shuttle *Dara*. She flew down the canyon, across the women's camp with its wagons and out across the valley toward Arad. The guard stepped out of the cave opening to watch the flight of *Dara*. He saw the vehicle hesitate briefly over Arad before it flew to the White Sea.

When *Dara* returned it flew slowly; two objects dropped. The guard saw a small package with a colored cloth fall onto the path outside the cave before it bounced and rolled down the slope and stopped above the river. A much larger package, a cloth sack wrapped inside a blanket fell onto the path and rolled a few feet.

The guard brought the large package into the cave and untied the cords holding the bag. He held up a light green fruit; it was an apple. The women quickly gathered around him while he counted 80 apples. Then he looked up at Harn and told him about the small package on the slope.

Celi opened her eyes, but slowly. After Eglan's baby was born she felt tired and meandered into a nap. She smelled onions and remembered where she was. She dreamed she stood with her arms straight out looking at Deem. She was happy for a moment; then she was afraid. Her dream faded into obscurity. She listened to the cave and heard silence.

When she turned her head she saw her friend Gran sitting, watching.

"We were told to let you sleep."

Celi said nothing. Under her large blanket she stretched and felt the small pains of unused muscles and began to sit up.

"We have apples," said Gran quietly.

"Apples?"

"*Dara* brought apples."

"And?"

"We wish to eat one. There are two for each of us."

Celi nodded and Gran slowly lumbered onto her feet. Her baby was close, the women believed. Her stomach was swollen tight inside her gowns. She wore a light blanket to keep warm. Gran walked toward the gathering of women and said, 'Yes!' with a bounce in her voice.

Her mate Harn brought an apple to Celi. He watched her admire the apple before he handed the small package to Celi. She looked at him with a question in her eyes.

"It fell," he said, meaning from *Dara.*

"You, me and Marl, outside," she said while climbing to her feet. Then she added, "No, wait!"

He turned back toward her; she opened the package. Celi unfolded a message painted onto a papyrus sheet. She scanned the sheet until she saw the name at the bottom, then gave it to Harn. Her face was blank; her eyebrows marched together into a frown.

The name at the bottom read 'Aonim' with the symbol for Captain. Harn saw more than felt her shoulders slump. "You thought..."

"Yes, from Deem."

He looked down at the message: *Stay in cave until ten days. Your camp, two horses dead. Arad, three dead. The camp near Sodom is a vast empty field of ash. Cities: Gomorrah, Sodom, Zoar nothing. The sea covers their evil. All the Lords, families evacuated from Shin'ar. Aonim, Cpn.*

"Arad, three dead," said Harn stating the obvious. "Talinda, her husband..."

"Yes," said Celi. She looked up at Harn, with expectation and fear in her eyes.

"You told me yourself that he trained Aonim to take over the *Dara.*

"An evil wind from the east," said Celi.

Harn looked at her.

"It means nothing good can come from the east. Shin'ar is in the east."

Harn made a small nod of his head. But a frown formed.

Harn stood and looked at her. Her eyelids came up sharply and she shouted "Stop eating! Now!"

The women turned to look at her. One said "Stop?"

"Yes," shouted Celi with authority. "Take all the apples and carefully wash them in our stream. That is my order from this day forward."

Chapter 37

The sun was behind the mountains to the west when Celi stood near the cave opening, watching the mountains to the east turn dark blue then black. *'You Lords,'* she thought, *'have the power. The Black Cloud came and you ran to the shuttles. Are you safe in a distant land? How could you abandon the sons and daughters you, . . .yes, . . .you created?'*

One of the women who worked by her side in the onion fields walked up and put her hand around Celi's hand. Together they stood and watched the canyon become dark. They saw the flash of a bat as it fluttered by their cave.

"You are worried? I think?" said the woman called Melan.

"It has been fifteen days. He never stayed away this long."

"Harn tells us that Deem no longer has the *Dara."*

"He is probably Second Captain of the *Cead* is my guess," said Celi. She knew *Dara* meant 'Second.' She also felt that Deem hoped to be First. *Cead* meant 'First.' It was the heavy shuttle with the blunt nose that entered the atmosphere like a leaf, flopping back and forth. *Cead* had the capacity to carry up to 40 passengers.

Melan squeezed Celi's hand. It felt cold. There was a visible sheen across her forehead. There were little beads of sweat across the visible top of her chest. Melan reached over and touched her side and felt moisture through the cloth.

"I bring wind from the east," said Melan. When Celi said nothing, she added, "Alim, the guard, is sweating. There are blisters around his stomach. He ran a hand through his hair and some of it came away in his hand. He asked me to apologize to you for him. He does not feel able to stand his work shift in the cave mouth."

Chapter 38

Celi looked down at Alim where he was wrapped in blankets. His hair was matted and wet. His pale face tried to mask the pain in his stomach. When he turned his head more hair pulled out and fell onto an old blanket he used for a pillow.

"You were a guard that first night after the bright explosion?

"The enormous flash and black cloud? Yes."

"You were in the cave opening?"

"Yes, Lady."

"We were all so tired. Harn thinks you were on duty all through the night. We forgot to send a replacement."

"Yes..." he began but something turned a vice in his stomach and his face turned white. A small groan escaped his mouth.

"Were you inside the entire night?"

"No. I was not," he managed to grimace between clenched teeth.

"You were not?"

"My mate was bringing water when you came and shouted at us to get down. She was on the slope to the river. You fell and I covered you to protect you."

"I fell?"

"Your voice had the sound of panic."

"And your mate?"

"She was gone."

"The air was black and full of small pieces of stone and sand and I do not know what else. I told everyone to stay out of the cloud."

"Yes, my Lady, you did." He coughed once, then choked on some saliva in his throat then coughed again. "I went out three times. Looking. Calling. The third time I went up the path with a torch.

"How long were you out?"

"A long time. Shouting her name. Looking. The sun was about to rise when I hurried back. You saw me come back. They were all sleeping."

"But you were in the canyon, breathing that air?"

"I held a cloth over my mouth."

"But not all the time?"

"No. I had to shout."

"I am sorry, Alim. There was a bad miasma inside the black cloud; you breathed it in."

"I know I am about to leave. Promise me something?"

"If I can?"

"Send a squad up the canyon and find her body."

"Her name was…"

"Surliann."

Celi bit her lip. The woman's name meant 'foul weather.' The name was equally applied to 'foul' mates.

Alim coughed again and a little blood leaked from his mouth.

"She was not that way. We only knew each other a short time. She was kind. She made pots and bowls in Arad. She was proud of her work."

"I will remember. We will erect a stone to you both."

The hint of a smile formed at one corner of Alim's mouth. He turned his head toward the cave stone and coughed. His hand moved and Celi took it to mean, *'Thank you,'* and she moved away.

Celi stood near the cave opening. Harn came up to tell her Gran was resting. The women thought her time was near. Lara wanted to help when the time came. Celi nodded at Harn and agreed. Gran was suffering from back pains and the baby needed to 'arrive' so the village could celebrate.

"You seem sad," said Harn.

"Remembering," she answered.

"It seems so hard to believe. Those enormous black clouds with the bright red eyes inside, almost as if it was a demon."

Celi had a flash of Málóid telling her she would see an angry black cloud above a city. *The red flashes made it seem angry,* she thought.

"It was. It killed. It destroyed. In one fast flash of death," said Harn.

"With all that has happened, I just now realized what *'the Lords evacuated'* might mean for Eridu."

"Mica's workers. My grandfather says they were ordered to make changes."

"Changes?"

"So the temple could serve Lord Mar.Duk."

"His workers. Do you think they died?"

"They would not be evacuated. Those who moved west probably died."

"Your grandfather is fortunate."

"We will raise a stone. Mica will carve it for us."

"They were gentle people. They had work and food for their families. I sometimes wonder how the Lords became so arrogant." Harn wore the face of frustration.

"You remember Misha?"

"My mother Cara and your Misha were cousins," said Harn.

"Did we ever meet?" she asked with curiosity.

"Misha would hold a gathering once every twelfth day. Or my Cara would hold the meeting to discuss our families. And there was food, much food."

"So we must have met?"

"I knew you. You were younger, and full of yourself, telling us you had *royal* blood as if we were not proper persons to meet you."

"I did?"

Harn smiled. He remembered the young girl who tried to tell others what to do. In those days he avoided her.

"I never talked to you."

Celi laughed. She smiled and laughed and put her hand on Harn's shoulder. When she closed her eyes she saw her Misha who died years in the past. She sobbed once.

"My lady?" said Harn with concern.

"They left Eridu. Left her to die," she said with true anger in her voice.

"The Lords, you mean?"

"Yes."

Harn watched her. He saw sadness in her face. He saw her concern for her pilot who was missing, or was he serving the Lords?

"We live," he said.

"That is true."

"We will remember," he added.

"Sand builds hills."

"My lady?"

"It is an old saying. We will build our village. Or we will move to another. We will build *our hill* on our memories and our growing families and those who join us."

"You are good for us," he said.

"Our stela. In the grove. We will add 'Eridu' to remember all the others who must have died when the royals fled."

"We could add a symbol…"

The pain died. She smiled, minutely. "…for the stoneworkers who died."

Chapter 39

A subtle sense of expectation prevailed within the cave. Five of the women were stitching baby wraps from a blanket. Two cooks were working on a stew made from the last of the horse meat. Celi felt cold. Two blankets were wrapped around her. Her feet felt cold. She touched her forehead. It was warm and damp. Melan came up to Celi and gave her a small bowl of water. Celi gulped it down.

"Gran is with the pains."

"It is about time she produces a baby from that enormous belly of hers," said Celi with a smile. "Who is with her?"

"Lara and Shene and my big, brave mate, Marl."

"Marl? What is he…?"

"He is showing Harn how to allow Gran to squeeze his hands through her pain. It is like some of the pain moves to her mate."

There was a long, slow scream from the isolated area of the cave. Three blankets were stretched over ropes to form a privacy wall. Celi glanced back toward the blankets.

"We have a new Aryas arriving," she announced forcefully.

"Oh! I forgot both parents are Aryas," said Melan.

There was silence for a long period. The women by the cooking fire continued stirring. By the cave entrance a small group was stripping bark off willow branches to make baskets with the strips. The silence was broken by the sound of a slap and a baby's plaintive wail that grew into an outright cry of protest.

From behind the blankets Lara announced, *'It's a boy!'*

"And his name shall be Harene," said Melan.

When Celi glanced at her, Melan added, "She told me."

"That is as it should be. You and Gran are good friends."

Melan stood for a moment looking down the cave to the blanketed area. She saw the sheen on Celi's forehead and knew Celi was running a fever. To herself she thought, *'Same fever that Alim has,'* but said nothing in the vain hope that perhaps her diagnosis was wrong.

"The Lady Celi states..." began Celi in a stentorian voice of authority, "we shall celebrate in Arad, our new babies."

Then she sat down quickly. Her stomach felt like the early stages of rebellion and dissent. In fact, she felt like she ate bad meat. She thought to summon Harn, her second in command but remembered where he was.

The woman who provided care to Alim for the past eight days straightened up and dried her hands on a towel. She stepped around boxes and large water jugs in order to walk toward the front of the cave. When she reached Celi, she said, "He has departed."

Celi thought for a moment and turned to Melan and asked her to record her words in the log of events of Arad: "It is a cycle. A man we cannot lose, dies. A baby boy joins our little village."

Chapter 40

"Does it bother you that I called the parents and baby Aryas?"

"No lady."

Melan looked at her mistress and added, "A whip makes no friends."

"Who told you that?"

"One of the big men at the mine. We called him Gnarly. He always had one side up, one side down on his mouth. Never happy. Always cursing. Using the whip."

"He told you that a whip makes no friends?"

"He told another big man. I thought it was a rule."

"A rule?"

"Beag work. Beag no talk. Beag look at ground," she paused. "Like that."

Celi was quiet while she thought about where Melan came from, the mines in the far south. Then she asked, "Are you happy, Melan?"

"Yes, Lady Celi. You call my name. Use no whip."

Celi thought about the mines. In Eridu there were stories when she was growing about men who asked '*...asked?*' she thought. *'More* *like fought for'* ...better treatment. She heard laughter when the person telling the story said, 'Yes, he was hung.'

When she thought about the men who told those stories she realized they were men who might have lost something, or lost position or lost a mate and blamed the Beag for their loss. They were men who grew up listening to others berate the Beag for their slow speech and inability to follow directions.

She remembered her tutor. When she asked her tutor why the Beag are so quiet she said, 'Beag no talk. They have nothing to say.'

Celi looked at Melan and asked, "In the mines how are the women treated?"

"Get fat, have baby, get more food. After baby comes the woman has light work for 60 days. They are called 'light' women. After 60 days their man returns."

Chapter 41

'C*eli in distress.'* There was word of mouth around the cave. The women knew she had a fever and rambled. For three days she cursed and swore, in the best traditions of the Aryas. Several times they heard her swear at Deem, shouting that he had no right to leave her here.

Mica sat by her side for part of each day. He sat and carved on a piece of hard wood. "Making a talisman," he said when asked.

When Harn tried to talk to her, she rambled on about onions and radishes and wheat and *'get that muddy dirt off your knees.'*

On the twelfth day after the 'Black Cloud' her friend Gran washed her face. She shared the duty with Sara, the 'maid' rescued from the Vizier in Salem. Gran reported to the rest of the women that her face was dry and she seemed to be sleeping, even snoring lightly.

The next day the sun was high overhead when Celi opened her eyes and slowly struggled to sit up. When Gran approached, Celi said simply, "There has to be food?"

Gran went and retrieved a bowl of stew from the cooking pot. The taste surprised Celi and she raised an eyebrow.

"There is rabbit. One of the men set traps far up the canyon when he saw small tracks. The black cloud did not affect the rabbit."

"Good. I eat."

Celi looked around the cave. Half the women were outside on the washing crew, hanging blankets on ropes strung between stakes. The remainder looked at her.

"How long was I asleep?"

Gran smiled at her and said, quietly, "Three days."

"How is your baby?"

"He sleeps. He drinks. He wets. He sleeps."

"That is good," said Celi. "I had this dream, just now, I think."

"A dream?"

"Yes, I was walking in an enormous field of onions. It stretched to the horizon where we had pens of sheep and a few horses. We are going to expand our fields. There are people who eat onions and radishes and sheep to the north of us, in Hebron and Jericho and Salem."

Gran smiled.

"And I felt angry in my dream..."

Gran put her hands together and began to rub the knuckles. Her hands appeared to be recovered from the work in the fields.

"Lady Celi, I will tell the others. You should rest." Gran began to smile and her smile broke into laughter. She reached over and touched Celi on her temple in a mark of respect.

"Any word? Or message from Deem?"

"No, none."

"That man is going to pay a heavy price when next I see him."

Gran opened her mouth to speak, but stopped. She smiled.

"She wants to argue," is how Gran described the irascible Lady Celi when she was asked later. "Wants to argue and chastise Captain Deem for being absent." When Gran was pressed, she admitted that Celi feared that Deem may have found himself puzzled and confused, under the spell of a wise, sly goddess such as Inanna.

Celi tried to bring herself to describe the beauty and soft smiles of the goddess Inanna, who she met once in Eridu. It was obvious the goddess had never toiled in a field. Her skin was flawless and darker than the skin of Deem. Her hair shone and reflected sunlight. Her white teeth reflected the beauty of the light reflected off the white limestone of Lord Enki's temple.

There was a saying among the women of Eridu. 'When the Goddess Inanna looks at a man he goes weak in the knees.'

Gran kept her own counsel, as a friend should. But Gran was older and had seen this behavior in the past in other women who did not know, yet, that they were carrying a child.

Gran did relay the wishes of Celi to the women. Three women and one of the guards volunteered to make the trek to Arad to bring back vegetables. They were told to fan the vegetables in the storerooms to get the dust off their surfaces. Have as little contact as possible. And wash the vegetables in the river before they bring them up from Arad.

Chapter 42

"We will stay up. We cannot land at Eridu," said Captain Deem to the four crew members on the control deck of the *Cead.* They were seated at their control stations, with their padded chairs swung around so they could see their Captain and look down on the Southern Ocean.

There were mighty clouds, white with gray below. The clouds seemed to boil up into large angry mountains of white and gray. Between the clouds *Cead's* crew saw a sea of deep blue or light turquois. They traveled north from the gold mines, bringing a load of ore to the smelter ovens far north of Eridu. His crew never grew weary of admiring the depth of the ocean.

"We will circle Eridu. I will tilt *Cead.* Tell me what you see."

They came in off the ocean and began to fly over the marshes south of Eridu. From the air they saw the canals and levees built by the engineers to control the water. They saw several patches of dry land where earth had been deposited when the canals were dug. They saw fields of crops, neglected and burning in the sun.

When *Cead* approached the sacred precinct of Eridu, they saw the Lord's high temple, a pyramid of four levels with a small square house at the top. There were no flags flying; the temple looked deserted.

They circled to the east, over the 'holds' as they were called. They saw a large pile of sheep, pushed up against a corner of the first hold, as if they tried to get through the gate of the corral. They were all dead.

From above the holds for horses and cows they saw horses lying on their sides. A small group of cows were crunched down on their legs, either sitting or lying on their sides. They were all dead, not moving, their legs extended into the air. There were three dogs tearing at the soft underside of the cows.

"Dogs," said a crew member,

"Hungry dogs," said another.

The *Cead* flew over the houses of Eridu. The men saw nothing. As they approached the market place one of the men groaned at the sight of men and women lying in the avenue. They seemed to be lying in postures that screamed with pain.

"I am glad we cannot see their faces," remarked Deem.

"Too sad," said another.

Deem turned the *Cead* into level flight. The crew was quiet. Not a word.

"I am the only one here who remembers Eridu as it was."

"Yes, Captain," said his Second.

"What did you see?" he asked his crew.

"Everything dead," said two of the crew.

"It is not what we saw, but what we did not see," said another.

"Yes," said Deem. "We did not see a single person standing."

The crew was quiet. Deem explained that he had been directed to fly over Ur, Lagash and Nippur on their flight to Bad Tibura, the city of smelters and tall smoke towers.

At all three cities the result was the same. The animals in the 'holds' were dead. The people were dead or not visible. On the roofs of the houses they saw little piles of black, blown into the corners by a wind. Wherever they looked they saw 'shadows' of black, where the wind deposited it.

"One of the princesses reported the cloud was black," said Deem. "A shepherd on the edge of Ur, west of Eridu, said the cloud came up over the mountains as if it was the Jin of Death."

"And it swept down on these cities?" said a crew member.

"Apparently. The royals had barely enough time to run north. They killed their horses in the mad dash to get north. Their sons and daughters had already been evacuated," added Deem.

"The gods were looking down with favor on them," said Second to his Captain.

"You missed the point," said Deem.

"And that was, Captain?"

"They knew what was about to happen before it happened."

There was silence on the crew deck. The *Cead* continued on her way to Bad Tibura, the city where gold ore was turned into ingots.

Chapter 43

Bad Tibura, when they saw it from the air, appeared to be alive. They saw smoke from two of the tall chimneys. They saw workers near the buildings that housed the smelters. As they crossed over the river they saw men unloading barges. They saw men on the pier at the river unloading the flat bottomed reed boats that were built to haul cargo from Punt, beyond the eastern sea.

"We heard the Pharaoh Hatshepsut was at Punt, two months ago."

"Aiyee, what a name," said a crew member.

"What did she want?" said another.

"Emeralds, rubies, carnelian, and opals. And gold ingots," said Deem.

"How did she pay?"

"With slaves for the mines of Abzu," added Deem. There was silence while Deem thought to himself, *and we received the task of moving them to Abzu.*

There was silence among the crew while Deem and his Second lined up *Cead*. They came down on a road north of the village and stopped near a building where a crew of men waited. The men wore trousers tucked into boots. They all wore masks across their faces. Several men held long handled brushes.

"We wash," said Deem.

He knew they were about to exit *Cead,* walk to the small tower where water was stored, drop their clothing and take showers. The clothing crew would bring white tunics and trousers. The 'ground' crew would wash and scrub *Cead* to make sure nothing of the 'black death' was on her.

"Tired of this cave, are we?" Celi laughed.

Harn, Gran and Melan stood around Celi where she sat on a stool with a blanket over her legs. They, as did all the women, hoped it was time to return to Arad.

"We go," added Celi, "when our squad is back. Lara and the two women and the guard can tell us what they saw. I suspect we will have to clean the roofs and walls of dust, and the floors inside also."

"I have a decision about Lara. She brought both babies. She earned the right to guide us in our health. I want her to go to Salem and seek training in the healing arts."

"She is not Aryas," said Gran with a frown, "and you have more than once displayed distrust for those of her kind."

"That was before this land was destroyed."

"We are the entire world," said Harn. "Will they allow her to be trained?"

"They must. I will send a decree." Celi looked across the cave and saw 'her' women were packing their few belongings. "These women have a role. They will make babies. Their mates will rebuild our world."

She paused. "I think I can trust Lara."

Chapter 44

"That miserable excuse! He left me with something I do not wish to have," said Lara, then added, "...before Char left."

"How do you know?" asked Celi.

"Shortly after the sun rises, I get up. My stomach is in revolt. This morning at our camp near the river what I ate came back up."

"That is a sign," said Celi thinking about Gran's description of her mornings in the early days.

Celi helped her loosen the thin ropes that held her load of onions, radishes, and a sack of barley. Lara's small squad returned from their long walk early in the afternoon. The other two women and the guard were talking to the other women about what they saw in Arad.

"The bodies were swollen," said Lara.

She watched Celi smell the bag of barley. One eyebrow went up.

"The guard Sem says mix some herbs with it, boil it good, then put it in a large jug to age, then add wheat ground into a paste."

When Celi frowned, Lara said, "Or something like that."

"Tomorrow, twelve of the women will go to Arad. The rest of us will stay here for seven more days."

Lara looked at the crowd near the cooking fire, where the women were animated and excited about 'walking down' to Arad.

"I want to go with them," said Lara.

"You and I will stay here for seven days. We must be careful. You are with child," added Celi.

"And you?" said Lara with a raised eyebrow and a smile.

Celi looked away for a moment. She watched the crowd of women and three guards while they milled around the cooking fire. One guard was busy eating from a bowl. The two women in Lara's squad were munching on an item that had no name. Wheat had been ground and mixed with herbs and let to sit until it became a spongy mass. Then dates and apple chunks had been inserted and the mass baked in a makeshift oven.

Lara asked her again, "And you?"

"I stay. I must be careful."

Celi turned back to Lara and held her hand for a moment. Then Celi released Lara's hand and smiled. "Your child ...it will be a treasure."

"You think so?"

"I do."

Celi looked out the mouth of their cave. The far side of the canyon was still in sunlight. A black shadow in the shape of the mountain behind her cave was slowly crawling up the far canyon wall.

"It will be dark soon," said Celi.

"And you will stay here for seven days?"

Celi turned back to Lara with a small smile and tilted her head toward Lara. "You must not say anything to the other women."

"About what?"

"I am having the sickness in the morning."

Lara looked at Celi then over to the group of women at the cooking fire. Lara gently squeezed Celi's hand and gave her the quiet smile of a co-conspirator.

Chapter 45

"It is appropriate," said Gran.

"That we stay?" remarked Celi.

"Yes."

They stood and watched the twelve women and Harn and one guard when they walked down the canyon. The women carried small bundles of possessions, blankets and clothes. Three women carried empty water jugs to fill and haul into Arad. The guard carried their only effective weapon, the hunting rifle that had served them these past sixteen days.

Across the valley the sun reflected off the White Sea and created a yellow and white landscape. High thin clouds streamed over the valley, pushed by a high wind from the west.

"Do you think it is safe?"

"The black cloud was here for what, sundown to middle night?"

"There could be poison," added Gran.

"Harn and the women will camp for three days by the canyon mouth," said Celi. "At the first sign of illness he is to begin the return to our canyon."

Gran reached up to pull the light blanket tight around her baby boy. He slept with a small smile on his lips, as babies do. She looked down and touched his pink cheek gently.

"There could be poison," said Celi. "Harn knows they must dust and wash everything and dispose of the wash water in a hole where it can be buried."

"The squad you sent with Lara. They told me there was very little dust or dirt on the buildings in Arad."

"The strong wind," Celi said. She watched the last woman in the line turn the last corner in the canyon trail and disappear from sight. "Still, there will be pockets of black poison on the roofs, in the corners."

"And the poison?"

"If it stays, we will move over the mountains toward Hebron and build a new town."

"You came from Eridu? What of the people who lived there?"

"They must have survived," said Gran hopefully.

They were silent. Celi and Gran bowed their heads and prayed for those who died.

'death roams the street, is loose in the road; stands beside a man, none can see it.'

(A Sumerian Memorial of Eridu).

Chapter 46

On the fourth day away from the cave, Harn and his squad of women moved into Arad, walking slowly and checking for black poison. They found small piles of dirt blown into corners between buildings. The buildings were clean, scoured by the winds from the west. Two of the women set up the water jugs on a stone altar near the small river. They worked to clean and scrub the Washing House; Harn insisted the women wash themselves each day.

On the fifth day away, *Dara* arrived. She came down gently, if such a word can be used, across the river. When Captain Aonim was asked he said he did not want to blow dirt back toward Arad. Landing in a field of wheat seemed like a sensible plan.

Harn and three women came out to meet Aonim. They took bags of apples, dates, figs, beans and lettuce back to their cook house. Harn remained behind, half expecting to receive bad news about Deem.

"No, Captain Deem is well. He is with the *Cead*." Aonim went to explain that both vehicles had been used to move the Lords to Abzu or to the land of the Great Pyramid. His mission was to bring news, to be helpful to the Arad village.

"How are the women?" asked Aonim.

"Twelve are here. Eighteen up the canyon at the cave. We are being careful. One of our guards died from the black poison," added Harn.

"The women are busy, working in Arad and up at the canyon?"

"You mean are they well?"

"Yes, I mean..."

"We have delivered two babies. They are showing the usual growth. There is one 'mother-to-be' at the cave."

"And that is?"

"Lara, the mate of Char. He 'caught' her after we left Eridu."

"That is indeed ...unfortunate."

Harn saw the pallor of regret crawl across Aonim's face. He knew what it meant. Harn waited a moment before asking.

Aonim looked out across the fields. "Char marched his men directly out onto the plains, near the landing site and the Army's wagons."

"We saw flashes of white light beyond the mountains. Down in Tilmun."

"Tilmun was the temple Lord Mar.Duk wanted to capture. He wanted to be ruler of all this land. Char and his men are dead, pulverized as one observer described it." [End Note 19]

"You have seen it?"

"What remains are small lumps of metal, melted wagon wheels, melted machinery, and smoldering piles of black rubble."

"Sand builds hills," noted Harn.

"Yes, he had sand. That man Char was a determined sort."

"I will tell his mate."

"Thank you. Tell her Captain, Lady Celi."

"I shall," said Harn with a small bow to Aonim for the information. He looked toward the small village of Arad and added, "Thank your Captain Deem for us."

"The Captain is fully occupied. They brought the *Cead* down. They sealed all the vents and added two air chambers. Captain Deem, I am told, put *Cead* on the bottom of the eastern sea at a depth of 100 cubits. It will be living and working quarters for men and women who want to live in the sea."

Chapter 47

"Working quarters?" said Harn.

"Oh, you do not know. *Cead* is south of Eridu, in the sea. Many of the Aryas wanted to live where the pull of the planet is less. They can harvest crops and fish and supply themselves in the sea.

Harn looked puzzled. "It is strange."

Aonim went on to tell him how the great Black Cloud crawled over the mountains to the east and killed everything in Eridu and Erech and Ur, where Enlil directed the affairs of his land. The war would not have happened had not Lord Mar.Duk acquired the support of the Hittite kings. Their men were the bulk of Mar.Duk's army, destroyed near Sodom.

"So much death," said Harn.

"Five great cities with their temples."

"What of Lord Mar.Duk?"

"He is a son to Lord Enki. They could not kill him."

"No, I meant where he is now?"

"Mar.Duk has abandoned his city; Babylon is dead."

Aonim looked out over the fields. He wondered how the Black Cloud would affect the crops but said nothing.

"They fled the cloud in a state of terror, those who are so quick to let the slaves in the Abzu mines die," said Aonim.

"You know about the mines?"

"You forget ...Captain Deem and I made several trips to Abzu, mostly delivering people to or from the mines."

"Ah..." mumbled Harn. He watched the women with their sacks of vegetables step out of the slow current of the river. "Good to wash."

"That is a standing order. Wash to get rid of the black dust."

"We have been lucky. Only one person dead at the cave. Here at Arad the old caretaker, his mate and their daughter died. Our horses died at our camp."

"Yes, I saw them dead. Nothing compared to Eridu or Ur."

"What did you see?"

"Many dead in the streets. Cattle dead in the stalls. Sheep dead and bloated in the sheep-holds."

"We hear some news from the stricken. Ningal, in Ur, went into an underground chamber. She complained that only cockroaches could live in that hole. One of her slaves pointed out to her that she was still alive to complain. She had the slave whipped.

"So the Lords and their ladies left their towns?"

"Lord Enlil we took to his pyramid on the Great River. He will direct 'his land' from there. His mate, Lady Ninki we took to Abzu in the south. Lady Inanna, the one they also call Ishtar, complained all during the trip that she had to leave her jewelry behind in Babylon."

"We are much obliged for your information," said Harn.

"And your Lady Celi?" he said with emphasis on 'Say-leest-Ay.'

"She is well."

"Good. I will send word to Captain Deem."

Chapter 48

A brilliant blue with scattered white clouds painted itself across the dome of heaven. In Eridu and Ur and Nippur and Babylon, the streets were empty and quiet. The few dogs that ventured in filled their stomachs with the flesh of dead cows; they died in two or three days. The streets and empty houses and the great temple in each city would remain empty for 70 years.

In the Land of Ekur, the Great Pyramid, the Lord Enlil now ruled with an iron fist. He approved promotions; his Council of Twelve rarely met. His technicians kept Ekur working to produce energy for the Anunnaki ships in space.

In Abzu, the mines and their slaves continued to work. The ore they sent north to Bad Tibura was smelted into gold ingots. Children pulled and pushed the ore carts. The older males dug ore in the tunnels. Abzu females worked in the fields; guards protected them from predators. An occasional child was lost to the lions or cheetahs. In the great southern continent, ore mined in the Andes was brought to Tiahuanaco and processed. [End Note 20]

In Abzu, one of the Anunnaki ladies was distressed over the failure to bring her jewelry south. Inanna asked for and received a slave, an old slave, to enter her apartment to retrieve her small chest with her jewelry. When Captain Aonim landed in Abzu he was directed to go to the Eastern Sea to retrieve Captain Deem, take Inanna (and her slave) to Erech briefly, and fly them both to the Temple of Isis, where Enlil was now Lord of the Land.

In Erech at ꭗAnu's temple the old slave walked into the dark, cavernous temple with a torch. After a long wait he re-emerged with a small chest. Inanna began to smile for the first time in 15 days. Captain Deem was about to pull the old slave aboard the *Dara* ramp when Aonim said, "Do not bother."

Deem looked at Aonim with an expression of incredulity. "Why?"

Behind Aonim, Inanna said, "Do not question him. He has his orders."

"Does he carry the black poison?"

"Probably on his clothes," remarked Aonim.

"So you will leave him in this vast dead city?"

"Yes," was all Aonim said as he hit the switch to close the ramp. He turned to Deem and remarked, "You are my responsibility. I take you and Lady Inanna to Ekur, by the great river."

The Great Pyramid of Enoch stood quiet in the late afternoon sun. Its bright white sheath of limestone slowly turned pink as Ra, the sun began to set in the west. [End Note 21] Directly east of the pyramid stood the Temple of Isis. Two guards and four priestesses bowed deeply when their goddess Inanna with Deem in tow approached the temple doors.

Inanna explained to Captain Deem that he was to meet with Lord Enlil in a few days. In the meantime, Inanna hoped to entertain him in her temple, the Temple of Isis. She said her temple women were the most beautiful; he was forbidden from touching any of the women.

Inanna instructed the woman called Renta to take Deem's bags with his uniforms and show him where he could change. She also suggested he change to a short tunic and sandals; she required an escort to the canal to wash. She was tired but would wash first.

The woman led Deem down a hall of white limestone. Light was provided by openings near the roof of the hall. They approached an arch with carved warriors on each side; a guard stood taller as they approached.

"Our blessed women, who earn tributes for the temple, live and sleep beyond those doors," said the woman as she led Deem past.

She walked past a doorway, turned to her left and gestured to Deem. He walked into a room filled with the smell of jasmine and lavender. There was a sleeping platform with a thick pad and two blankets, folded on the pad. An ancient wooden chair stood in a corner. A small vase with a spring of lavender sat on a table near the chair. Deem looked up and saw there was no roof. Light came from the openings in the hall. When the woman put Deem's bags down, he said,

"I am expected to sleep in this cabin?"

Renta smiled. She raised an eyebrow. "That is not its real purpose."

Deem said nothing. He waved her out and began to undress.

Deem finished tying his sandal straps moments before Renta reappeared. She had changed into a light robe and carried what looked like four towels and washing cloths and soap. She asked Deem to follow

her. They went farther down that same hall, turned twice and walked through a doorway into bright sunlight.

"Lady Inanna will come here. You will escort her down to the canal."

Deem said nothing. He almost bowed to Renta.

Moments later Deem heard footsteps in the hall. An enormous guard with a curved ceremonial knife stepped into the sunlight. Behind him came Inanna. She wore an enormous white robe with arms that reached her wrists. The robe had a collar as wide as a hand. She wore a thick belt of black cloth with gold emblems around her middle. She stepped up to Deem and said, "By my side."

Together they walked the slope down to the canal. This was the canal that brought stone and quarry products up to the base of the temple during its construction.

"You are privileged," said Inanna.

When Deem said nothing, she added, "You are privileged to be allowed to walk this close to my side."

When they reached the canal Inanna continued to walk, stepping slowly into the almost clear water. "It is not always this clear."

Deem stopped and watched her. When the water reached her waist, she stopped. Inanna pulled the lower part of her robe up until it floated. Then she pulled her arms out of her robe and allowed the robe to fall around her waist. To Deem she said, "Drop your tunic so it does not get wet. Bring me the washing cloth and the soap."

Renta stood behind him. He turned for the soap and towels then realized he would need to drop the strap around his waist.

"My lord, I have done this many times," said Renta.

Deem turned away from her, undid the strap and handed his tunic to Renta. He turned toward the water and stepped into the canal. He was conscious of his naked condition in front of these two women.

When he reached Inanna with the soap she asked him to scrub her back. His footing became a little uncertain. He reached out and put his hand on her back to steady himself.

"That is not your privilege," said Inanna.

"Trying to stand," he said.

She turned half-way and put her hand on his shoulder. He was aware of her breasts and she said, "Beautiful, am I not?"

Deem stood, as if struck by lightning. When he said nothing, Inanna asked,

"Do you desire me?"

"No, my lady."

"No? Can you not say more?" She took the washing towel from him and began to wash herself. She gave Deem the towel and he washed her back without touching her skin. She used water to run her fingers through her hair. After she was satisfied she turned toward the beach and Renta. As she walked away she told Deem to ask Renta to guide him back to his small room. "Renta will come for you when our meal is properly prepared."

Chapter 49

Deem dressed in his black trousers with the red side-stripe. He wore his red uniform jacket over a white cotton shirt. He slicked his hair with oil; he shaved with his trusty blade. *Taken as a sum,* he thought, *I must look rather handsome.* He spread oil with jojoba and cedar wood scent across his face. But then he frowned. *This goddess, this Inanna, she wants to impress Lord Enlil with her prowess?*

There was no answer to his question. The servant Renta brought Deem to Inanna's private quarters. She made him wait outside two old wooden doors; he straightened his uniform jacket. *They make me wait?*

When Renta opened a door Deem stepped into a long hall with a high ceiling. The light was dim; he saw woven cloths on the walls. Seven candles burned in an iron device shaped like a five-pointed star. Along one wall there were candles held in small holders suspended from tree limbs that leaned away from the wall murals. As his eyes adjusted he saw the sleeping platform held posts at the corners with thin white cloth suspended from cords. *Where is she?*

Then he saw Inanna. She stood in a far corner draped in a long robe of white. Her hair was up, swirled above her head. She wore the black accents of a goddess below her eyes. Because the corner was dark Deem could barely see the smile on her lips. She spoke to a servant and the door behind her opened. The room was bathed in the bright yellow of the setting sun.

The effect was stunning. The light shone through her robe. Her legs were exposed as if she were naked. Inanna raised her arms and half-turned. Deem saw one breast outlined with the sun behind it. She glanced at Deem for a moment and lowered her arms.

"What do you say, Pilot?"

Flustered, he said nothing. *What?* flashed through his mind.

After several moments of quiet an old phrase that Captain Shar taught him when he began training tumbled off his lips. "I am at your service, my lady."

"At my service, you say?"

"Yes, my lady."

Deem turned away from the vision of Lady Inanna when one of her guards brought a table and put it near the foot of her sleeping platform. This man was one-half head taller than Deem and massive. The guard left and quickly returned with two chairs. Behind him came Renta with a platter of dates, broiled mutton, and pieces of beef swimming in a sauce.

Inanna quietly walked to Deem and put a hand on his elbow. "When Renta returns with a knife I expect you to cut a piece for your goddess."

Deem felt heat in his cheeks. He was aware of her robe and how it fell to her waist. A breast was partially exposed.

"My lady?" He felt her hand travel from his elbow, across his back. He was aware of the lavender scent of her.

Renta brought two knives and two forks; she placed a jug on the table. Deem retrieved a knife, held the meat and sliced a morsel. Inanna took a fork and bent over to spear the meat. As she did her breast was fully exposed. Deem felt her hand travel down to his buttock.

He straightened up. In one motion he waved the knife in her direction and said, "What is it you expect of me?"

She looked at the knife and pushed it away. She said nothing while she pulled her robe together; she looked at the piece of meat and said, "We must eat ...first."

First? occurred to Deem. He watched her nibble on the meat while she walked around the table. She turned and sat on a chair. Her robe fell between her legs.

This woman ...has no sense of hiding her body from a man.

She continued to chew her meat strip. Deem watched her for a moment before he asked,

"What is it you expect?"

Renta suddenly reappeared with two bowls. She pulled the stopper from the jug and poured a grape mixture into each bowl. When she turned to leave Inanna said harshly, "Do not try my patience, Renta. Bring the bowls first next time. Tell this man what I expect of him."

Renta stopped to say, "She expects nice words; she expects you to praise the goddess of love and war; she wants you to perform on her platform."

"What?" escaped from Inanna's mouth.

Renta's face went blank. The frown on Inanna's face may have scared Renta.

"Renta ...where did you get the impression ...from who?"

"From you, my lady."

"From me?" said Inanna. The Goddess slowly said, "This is beyond belief."

In shock, or total confusion Deem said nothing. He stood and looked at these two adversaries knowing that Inanna held 'life and death' authority over Renta. Deem brought his hand up and rubbed his forehead. He knew stress usually induced a mild headache. He looked at Renta, then Inanna and slowly said,

"Renta ...echoes your behavior ...she sees how you dress."

Deem saw an eyebrow raise and added, "Lady, you asked her."

"Did I?" began Inanna. "Yes, I guess I did have Pilot Deem on my mind. You are so ...so ...pleasant to look at."

"Thank you, my lady."

"Renta, you are excused. Report to the Temple Women for training."

While Renta walked to the door out of her lady's presence, Deem asked, "What do you mean ...training?"

"She has reached far beyond the age of Beginning. She was eligible to serve the temple, perhaps three years ago. It is time she begins to serve."

"So you punish her?"

"Do I what?"

"Punish her? For speaking her mind?"

"It is not punishment. She can stop serving me and learn how to serve men and their desires. She can tell stories of the Lady Inanna and her love for Dumuzi, who died. She will eat well, work little, and occasionally enjoy the arms of a man around her."

"Is that what you expect of me?"

"You are brash Pilot Deem."

"How am I brash?"

"That you have the courage to ask me what I expect of you?"

"What is it?"

"I expect you to fill a void in my life, even if only briefly. Then I will urge Lord Enlil, my master and yours, to promote you to Captain of the *Rama*, a Deep Black vehicle that approaches."

Deem stood without moving. Inanna reached out and speared the piece of beef and pulled it toward her. She began to slice another thin slab.

"My Lady," said Deem. "It is time. The sun has gone into the west on its journey and will return from the east."

"Time for what, exactly?"

"Time for me to return to my quarters."

Inanna sat and chewed a piece of meat. "Did I say you were excused?"

She sat and watched as Deem passed through the door and into the middle redness of early evening. He was thinking about Captain Shar's rule for achieving success as a pilot: *You make the decision. You live with it. You do not allow the Lords to tell you how to behave. You are a pilot, a bird of the sky.*

Chapter 50

A brilliant blue painted itself across the dome of heaven while Ra rode his chariot across the morning sky. The sun shone down on fields of onions, radishes, barley, melons, beans and wheat. Despite the nuclear disaster, the fields planted in early spring by the Beag men flourished and grew and turned a deep green in mid-summer.

The days grew warm. Light breezes caressed the mountains to the west and brought strong winds down the canyons. Arad basked in the sunlight; a light rain washed the buildings. Celi kept her women busy; they used digging sticks to rid the fields of weeds. The women enjoyed the sound of the two new babies who let everyone know when they were hungry.

The three men, their remaining guards, found mates among the women. There was some jealousy among those left alone when their men did not return from the Restricted Zone. Celi, when she was told of this, issued a rule with the force of law. She ruled that Harn and two men would go to Hebron to recruit men for the women. She also ruled that 'those left alone' will not talk nor entice the men who have mates. To break this rule could result in banishment.

This day would be remembered in the future for the brilliant blue sky and the dark animal who wandered into their onion field and began eating onions.

Ashur, Eglan's mate stood next to Marl, the guard on duty. They stood atop a small building where they could survey the fields. Ashur regaled Marl with stories about his baby girl and her behavior during the dark night. Ashur was grateful his baby girl was beginning to sleep all during the dark; she woke up hungry at first light.

To Marl the black mass appeared to be a small bear, crawling into the onion field at the far eastern corner of the field. There was long black hair on its head; its body was covered with a short fur. Then the animal turned and Marl saw its hips had no fur; in fact, it was a man of dark skin with a fur wrapped around his body.

When he asked Ashur to look his friend stared at the black mass and agreed that it was indeed a man with long hair. They both wondered why he crawled on the ground. When Marl saw two women at the north end of the field turn in his direction, he decided he must get the rifle and go to protect them from the dark man. He asked Ashur to inform Lady Celi that there was a man in the onion fields.

Marl dragged the man, forcing him to walk out of the onions and into Arad. When they stopped the man fell to his knees. Marl said "Here he is."

Celi looked at the man where he knelt with a light rope tied around his neck. He was bent over; his long black hair had streaks of gray; his hair hung down over his face. His hands and feet were covered in the light tan earth of the onion field. A ragged fur with small holes covered his body. His skin color was dark; his brow had a prominent ridge. There were blisters on his nose.

"You …are Beag. Get up …up," said Celi with a gesture to stand up.

The man tried to bring his head up. His shoulders went back. His face was covered with gray hair. He stood with effort. His eyes looked at her briefly then back at the ground. His legs were not straight; they remained bent.

"Up," she commanded.

The man bent his back, tried to straighten himself. His head came up slightly before he looked at Celi a second time.

"He was injured, I think," said Harn from behind the man.

She looked at his legs where they bent at the knee.

"Too dark for Beag," said Celi.

"He is Adamu, born after the sons and daughters rebelled and demanded workers for the mines," said Harn.

"What is he…?" she began but stopped. She looked at Harn and Marl and Melan and the three women who formed a circle around the man. She bent over to look into his face and said, "Who? Who?"

The man reached up and pulled a thin rope from inside his wrap of fur. The rope was threaded through an old wooden plaque. It held the symbol Ṝ.ώ which puzzled Celi. She pointed at Ṝ, the man said, "Ren."

She pointed at the symbol of the double horns and he raised one eyebrow. Harn moved forward and leaned in to stare at the symbol.

"Double horns, sign of Osiris, the Bull. The other marks say twelve, that means twelve generations from Osiris."

"How do you?" asked Celi.

"I asked the Lord at the second mine we visited," said Harn. "Much later Deem warned me to not ask many questions, as he put it."

"This man is from...?"

"The mines of Abzu," finished Harn.

Celi waved her hand in front of the man's face. He took his eyes off the leather sandals on Harn's feet and looked up at Celi.

"How?" she said loudly and waved her arm around then pointed at the ground. The man looked at her for a long moment. Then he pointed in the direction of the White Sea and said, "Sleep. Sleep. Two sleeps. Lord tell me walk toward my shadow."

"He came from the east," said Harn.

"What did you see?" said Celi.

The man looked puzzled and said, "I work, Mistress. I work."

She pointed to her eye and mimicked looking around.

The man raised his hand and moved it, as if across a flat landscape. He stopped the movement and said, "Dirt, Mistress. All dirt." He looked up at her and added, "Bones. Heads. No skin."

She looked up at the White Sea in the distance. Sunlight bounced off the surface. The glare seemed to turn the sea and the land to the south into a white miasma.

"Do you suppose?" she began. Then she looked at Marl and told him to take the man to the river and wash him and burn the decrepit fur thing he wore. She told two of the women to bring some trousers and a wrap from the house of the man who died after the explosions. When they left she told Melan and the two women to go to the cooking house and prepare simple food.

"It is a waste," said Harn.

"Why?"

"Marl said his mouth voided itself of the onions he ate. There was blood in his half chewed onions."

To the man Ren she said, “How many days?”

When he did not answer Harn waved his arm across the sky and raised one finger, then two, then three, then four.

The man suddenly bobbed his head. “Four,” he said. “Four crossings the sky.”

Celi nodded her head. “Yes, four days,” and meant four days he walked from the ruins of Mar.Duk’s army. She looked at Ren and said, “Your mate? You had a mate where you worked?”

The man nodded his head and held it down while he looked at the flowing gown Celi wore. He raised his head to say, “Mate. She work. She gives…” and he held up one hand to indicate ‘five’ “…workers. She dies.”

“So your mate had five children …no, workers?” The man did not reply. Celi told the man Ren to go with Marl. She saw two of her squad walking toward the river with clothes and soap and a large towel and directed, “Do not touch him.”

The man Ren began to turn. Harn suddenly shouted stop and walked over to Ren. He bent over to look at the backs of Ren’s legs. Harn took a long moment to inspect the back of the man’s knees. Then he waved a hand at Ren and told him to “Go” with Marl.

Harn watched them walk toward the river. His shoulders slumped, head down. He did not look at Celi until she said, “What?”

“His legs are bent for a reason.”

Celi said nothing.

“They cut the backs to keep him from running.”

Celi said nothing. She turned away and looked back at her small village with its white temple shining in the afternoon sunlight.

“Do you suppose…?” she began.

“Lady Celi, I do not suppose. I know. One of your…” he paused, trying to find a word, “…rulers, or Great Rulers, *or his scribe* chose that man. They put him down where the Brilliance of Enlil destroyed the army of Mar.Duk. He saw skulls and bones and dead vultures."

"They wanted to know..." she began. Harn finished with "...if he would live."

Chapter 51

Mid-summer. Days of high heat. The field workers began to pick the largest of the onions and radishes, leaving the smallest plants to continue their growth. The barley they brought to the oven where it was baked until a hard brown then ground to fine powder, mixed with yeast and allowed to age in a large clay pot with water. The field workers began to bring in melons and beans to be eaten as they matured.

The men were sent to dig silt out of the main canal when the river level began to drop. There had been little rain on this side of the mountains but the river out of the canyon continued to provide what they needed.

The man called Ṝen lived for another six days. He ate what he could between bouts of enormous cramps in his stomach. His screaming woke the entire village several times in the long black nights.

The shuttle *Dara* came down just after sunrise on a crystal clear morning. Aonim marched stiffly, as if afraid of the ground and the buildings and stopped in front of the tall wooden doors of Lady Celi's temple. One of the women informed Captain Aonim that the man Ṝen was dead. Aonim stood and waited. A woman brought him a bowl of light green juice. When informed it was 'juice from a large fruit' he sniffed the juice, wrinkled his nose and returned the bowl to the woman.

The woman stood and smiled at Aonim. By now five other women had arrived. He glanced at them and they also smiled. Time passed slowly for the Captain of the *Dara.* When Celi stepped through the door of her temple, she was radiant with energy. Aonim later described her as a beam of sunlight that outshone the early morning sun.

She wore a long flowing gown that reached just above her sandals. Her dark hair was lighter, bleached in the sun. Her hair was long now, uncut but wavy with curls each side of her face. Her stunning face reflected the weight of the decisions she had made. A woven shawl wrapped her shoulders and most of her body. Celi's blue eyes cut through Aonim when she examined him. She noticed a twitch in his hand.

"You must eat. We have fried fish and boiled beans."

Aonim bowed toward Celi and thanked her but refused her invitation. When he said he was told not to touch anything, by way of explanation, Celi reacted with "You tell them we are alive here."

She looked at Aonim to see if he understood her words, then added, "Your marker, that worker you set down in the devastation, has died."

"I am to bring his body to Salem. The doctor wants him."

"So be it," said Celi through clenched teeth. "We do not want to do anything contrary to the wishes of the Royals who fancy they are gods."

Chapter 52

It was a cool morning. The women stood around Celi and Aonim and listened. Gran stood back behind Celi and watched her. Gran had watched Celi in recent weeks. She saw a growing sense of sadness inside the weak smiles of her friend. Gran remembered the days her mistress had been joyful, the days when Deem visited Arad just about once each week for a night. They were the days before the Black Cloud. And now two months had passed with no sign of Deem.

Aonim looked at Celi with a raised eyebrow. He looked puzzled. Then he added, "I am to tell you Deem is at Ekur, the great white pyramid. He sent you those apples and dates which my crewman Ragnar is bringing off the *Dara.*"

Celi made a small bow as a sign of appreciation. Ragnar, the crewman from *Dara,* passed by with two large sacks. He walked to the two women who stood by the Cooking House and began to talk to them. One of them reached out to caress the fine-spun quality of his uniform jacket. He glanced at Aonim who pointed at the *Dara.* The message was clear.

"Will you take a message to Deem? My words, only?"

Aonim nodded and she said in a quiet voice, "Captain Deem, if you intend to remain a pilot, do not return to Arad." Aonim raised an eyebrow for a second time, but nodded yes, he understood.

Celi then directed him to take a load of onions and radishes and Harn to Salem, for trading. She dismissed Aonim with a wave of her hand and turned to step into her temple, where the cool air gave her a chill.

She wrapped her arms around herself and rubbed her arms against the chill air. Then she bowed her head, and said a silent prayer to any god who would listen. After a short moment she looked up and saw Gran watching her from just inside the tall doors of the main room.

As Gran crossed the room she said quietly, "Was there word of Deem?"

"Yes," Celi began with bitterness on her tongue, but quickly looked through a high window at blue sky and remarked that they should get their tasks finished before the heat of the day rolls in.

When Gran was asked later by two of her friends, she noted that her Mistress seemed to be sad or quiet or angry or all three. She also noted that Lady Celi hid her swelling belly under the thin cloth coat that fell to her feet.

Relief from the heat arrived quietly in late summer. A cool breeze meandered down the canyon and enveloped Arad in a blanket of cool relief. In the mountains heavy gray clouds began to dump their cargo of rain into the mountains. To the people of Arad, it was a blessing. Their river from the canyon had shrunk to half its size. The water would be welcome for the fields and somewhat cooler for washing.

It was several days after the visit of the *Dara* before Lara decided to ask about Deem. Her question brought silence. Celi stood and looked out across the valley to where the White Sea was covered by gray masses of cloud. Out of the silence Celi said, quietly,

"Could he tell? Did I look thin?"

"You mean?" began Lara.

"You were off to one side. Could he see my stomach?"

Lara was silent, trying to formulate an answer. "Men are somewhat like a heavy cream about these things. Slow to pour, sweet when they need to be."

"He will tell Deem I am the mistress of Arad?"

"Aonim is an obedient servant of the Aryas."

Celi looked out across the fields, then at the three women who just returned from the fields. Her hand touched her stomach with a caress.

"We will build what we want to build. We will get more men. We will have more babies. We are Aryas."

When Lara remarked that she was mixed blood, not pure Aryas, her mistress said, "We can make a better world; a world better than what our lords and their 'so-called gods' has created, with its wars and Black Death."

Chapter 53

Late summer in Arad. The heat was moderated. The crops were in harvest. Lady Celi and her advisors were talking about planting a second crop of onions and radishes to see if they would grow in the well-watered fields.

It was no longer a secret that the short woman named Lara was 'with child' and her mate Char probably died in the war. A few women, when they heard the name 'Char' had developed a habit of spitting on the ground to express their displeasure with Lara's mate, dead though he may be.

It was also no secret that their mistress, Lady Celi was trying to hide the fact that she was 'with child' and the women of Arad believed Deem was to blame. They had stopped calling him Captain. Some said 'after all he is not where he should be.'

The Great Pyramid was now called Ekur, the Temple of Lord Enlil. The ancient lord had returned to the land of the decrepit crouching lioness called the Sphinx when Ur and its people died from the Black Poison. There was no word of Lady Ninki.

Harn brought word from Salem that *Cead* had been allowed to sink into the eastern sea. It was now serving as a base for some of the Aryas who were living in the vehicle. They were fishing and farming on the shallow sea floor and beginning to understand what they could achieve under the water. The few survivors of the Black Cloud on the shore brought offerings of fruits and vegetables for the enormous 'fish creatures' that lived in the sea.

The *Cead's* pilot was ordered off the *Cead* when it was noted that his mate was not with him. He was brought to the Temple of Isis, next to the Great Pyramid, where he met Lord Enlil, the Commander of the Four Regions of Earth. Deem, a distant grandson of Enlil, was puzzled. Enlil asked Deem to be patient; one of the pilots and his family were about to relocate and move to a northern island in the western sea. [EndNote 22]

Enlil told Deem he was eligible to become the next pilot of the *Rama,* named in honor of Enlil's half-brother Enki.

Deem was stunned. He bowed in reverence to the mighty lord. He took three steps to back away from Enlil. He thought immediately of the long months he had been away from Arad. It had been too long. He had served and was tired of his work as a pilot.

The aged, somewhat infirm Enlil noticed Deem's action and believed his young pilot was rejecting the offer. "Are you unsure?"

Deem stood silent. *'How do I answer him?'*

From the back of the temple room, Lady Inanna, Goddess of Isis, moved to stand next to Deem. When Enlil asked if they were mates, Inanna replied, "Not today, my Lord." The un-spoken words implied that they could soon be mates.

Chapter 54

The sun began to touch the mountains west of Arad. The shadows of the Blue Mountains crawled across the valley floor; Arad turned dark in the shadows. The last bit of sunlight lit the tall pole Mica erected in front of Lady Celi's temple.

A flag fluttered in the light breeze. The women used a tightly woven sheet on which they stitched an enormous letter 'O' next to a smaller letter 'm' with a band of green cloth below the two letters. The symbol stood for 'Ninki' whose title was 'Lady Life.' The women were asking Ninki to watch over their village.

Celi also pointed to the symbol and said 'O'magadh' which is an old expression when you do not believe what a man is telling you. "You say 'O'magadh' which means '*Oh, Really?*' in our old language."

Several of the women laughed at her irreverence.

When Celi and Lara walked back into the temple, Celi pulled Lara aside and said, "Are you happy?"

"You mean, I believe, do I wish I had a man?"

Celi said nothing. She knew Lara was stubborn. She was a hard worker in the washing house.

"You know," Celi began, "I feel a pain when I think about you."

"It is what it is," said Lara. An image of Char when he was angry flashed through her mind. She felt a small movement inside her belly and smiled. She touched her bulging stomach. Celi did the same, on the distinct curve in Celi's stomach.

"We have our babies," said Lara.

Celi wrapped her arms around Lara, briefly. She released her then looked into her eyes and said, "We reap the harvest of sadness."

"A harvest caused by men," added Lara.

Lara saw tears form in Celi's eyes; Lara turned away.

Chapter 55

It was quite by accident that Lara began to fall for the older carver of stone, the man Celi thought of as 'grandpa,' her Mica. Lara had accepted the job of washing and hanging towels outside the Washing House. It was not the most difficult of jobs; she felt she must contribute to their community. Lara was collecting towels when Mica walked into the room where the washing pool stood. She was flustered; he was breaking the rule, she thought.

"The wood is stored outside," she quipped.

"You mean the wood is?" said Mica.

"Outside. Near the fireplace that heats our water."

"Ah, I see."

"Do you, old man?"

Mica looked at her. Lara wore an old pair of trousers she used for work in the fields. Her tunic was tight around her body. She held towels in front of her stomach. Mica was shocked by the quality of her smile. It was large; she mocked him, he thought. Her hair was wrapped in a turban; her eyes caught Mica's eyes. He felt compelled to smile back at her.

"And you are?"

"I am Mica. The carver. Lady Celi asked me to install steps into the shallow end of this washing pool."

"To be greatly appreciated by the women,"

Lara walked to the shallow end and stood next to Mica. She watched him use his cubit stick to measure the width of the shallow end. He decided he must dig outside the pool and install stone steps that rose to the pool floor, but outside the pool itself.

Standing next to Lara the stone carver was impressed. "Are you not afraid of me?"

"Of you, Mica?"

"I have permission to be here."

"My friends tell me you are Lady Celi's father."

"More like her honorary father."

"She has no father?" Lara was puzzled.

"You are a nice person, Lara," added Mica. He turned and walked out of the Washing House. Lara, in later days, remarked she was glad to have met a polite, and proud man who took his work seriously. They began to meet in the morning while Mica worked on digging out the corner of the pool. One day he brought a baked item for her. While resting he told her about 'his Misha' and their life with Celi. *We could be comfortable;* she began to think.

Chapter 56

Four guards in royal red uniforms marched imperiously up to the main doors of Lady Celi's temple in Arad. The morning was new; the sun barely over the distant mountains beyond the sea. One of the guards used a short staff, a wooden weapon used to make inquiries among prisoners when they are reluctant 'enemies.' He rapped three times on the doors to the temple.

There were neither women nor guards about this early in the day. The four guards stood in casual rest and waited. The original guard hit the door with four loud bangs from his staff. He stepped back to wait.

They were young, thin men with black hair and the pale skin of the Titans, the hand-picked guards of the Lords. Each of them had the straight nose of the Aryas, and the deep black eyes of royalty.

One of the guards coughed. When the leader looked at him the guard nodded toward what the women called the 'Washing House.' They saw a face peering from behind the door.

The guard yelled, "You. Come here."

There was silence from the Washing House. The door slammed shut. The four guards had no time to react. They turned in unison toward a second group of four guards as they approached. Behind them walked a man of exalted rank. His red tunic reached his knees. He wore sandals with leather straps wrapped around his calves. His face was severe; his demeanor impatient. He wore the rank of Major, a silver circle with seven green gems inside the circle.

His skull was bare on the left side. From the midline of his skull his long black hair had been pulled over his right ear and woven into a black rope that hung to mid-chest. He looked at the guards and said, "Nothing?"

"No, my Lord," said two of the guards in unison.

At that moment there were sounds of a heavy beam turning inside the temple doors. The sounds stopped. They heard a latch slide and the right hand door began to creak and groan as it was pushed outwards. A woman in a dark blue gown with a shawl around her shoulders leaned outward around the door. She saw the group of men in red tunics. Beyond them she spotted the shuttle. *Dara's* captain Aonim and one crewman stood near the exit ramp of the shuttle.

"My Lord," said one of the guards "requires a meeting with your mistress, Lady Celiste of Arad."

The woman turned and disappeared. The men stood for a long moment while a frown formed on the face of the Lord. He eventually said, "So open the door," and indicated the nearest guard. The guard moved quickly, pulled the door open then bowed in deference as the Lord entered.

Celi sent her maid to fetch Harn and his squad, which had swollen to six men recently. She told her maid Sara to say, *"A royal at the temple. Your best uniform would be appropriate."*

Celi spent time with her hairbrush to pull the snarls out of her hair. She washed quickly in an effort to get the tired feeling out of her face. The entire community worked hard the previous day to remove all of the full onions and radishes from their fields. The men, meanwhile, harvested the barley. Today they were to beat and sort the barley heads.

She found her long white gown, rarely used lately. There had been no one to entertain. She wrapped the gown around her body and secured it with a cloth belt. Into her hair she mounted three yellow blossoms. She carefully placed her chain with its ankh around her neck. The symbolic circle above the 'T' rested on the mid-line of her chest. Then she wrapped a bright red necklace around her neck and tucked it under the silver ankh.

She turned to look at herself in a burnished mirror just as her maid announced Harn and his squad were at the side door into the temple.

Celi walked into the main meeting room then crossed to the side door. She allowed Harn to marshal his men into the large room. Behind the altar they formed a single line in a half-circle. Her maid Sara brought a spring of evergreen and placed it on the 'almost dead' embers on the altar. A whisk of white rose toward the ceiling. Only then, when her men were ready, only then did she look up to see the elegant man in his long red tunic with its badge of rank.

He took two steps away from his guards. His red tunic reached to his knees. On his left shoulder he wore a silver circle with seven gems that declared he was from Lord Enlil's court. He was not clean shaven; a beard of black with gray traces covered his chin. His eyes were dark in the shade of thick eyebrows.

She walked between her men then stopped next to Harn. Two of the other man's guards had weapons on their belts, the kind of weapon that fires a pellet of iron. She pointed at one of the weapons then glared at their leader.

"You insult the house of Ninki, our goddess."

The man looked at his two guards and said, "Remove your weapons."

To Celi he said, "They are effective weapons from our engineer."

"This is good," said Celi slowly. "We accept them as tribute."

"But these are…" began one of the guards.

The man's fist came up in a blur of motion and smacked the guard on the side of his face. The guard reacted by staggering for one step, then he stopped. He removed his shooter and gave it over. Harn took both weapons and placed them on a table near Celi.

"We accept your apology, and your tribute. We are but a small village and our children will thank you for helping to protect them." At the end of her speech she bowed to the man.

"You will accept the two weapons as apology for the bad behavior of my men, I expect."

Celi smiled and looked at the guards. "Your men may withdraw. We will do no harm to you."

The man looked at her briefly then waved at his guards and told them to wait outside. When they turned toward the large wooden doors Harn motioned to his men to withdraw. Harn moved back to where he could intervene if needed. He felt responsible for the safety of Mistress Celi.

"You may explain to me…" began Celi.

"…why I am here," finished the man. He took one step toward Celi and then stopped. "I am the one you never knew."

"Never knew?"

"I was prevented from traveling to Eridu while you were growing. I so much wanted to share my life with you. Your grandfather Mica was a good man."

Celi paused then asked, "You said was?"

"Was he not in Eridu when…?"

"No. One of your pilots found Mica walking west and brought him here."

The man stood. An eyebrow moved, as if he questioned what he heard.

"He is a good man."

"Yes," added Celi.

"Was he asked to work on Mar.Duk's temple?"

"Yes. He refused."

Chapter 57

Celi stood and looked this man up and down. She saw his red tunic and his badge that literally shrieked 'Anunnaki' and 'Family of Enlil.'. And she felt his sense of arrogance.

"Did Mica prevent you from coming to Eridu?"

"Not your grandfather, I assure you. It was Lord Enlil's decision. He ruled my 'indiscretion' prevented me from returning to Eridu."

"You followed his order?"

"Yes. I am a man of another world. I love my land and its mines and its temple. I am only here briefly in Salem. We brought twelve barges north with ore to the smelters. I chose to ignore Enlil's order. In thirty days we will board *Rama* and leave for the home planet."

"My grandfather Mica described you."

"Yes. I am Seth.Dar."

"My Misha never said a word about you."

"She was... how to say it ...angry but quietly excited. She knew your mother Elanna."

"She died in an accident."

"Yes."

"She was as beautiful, if that is possible, as her sister Inanna."

Celi stared at him. "This Inanna, is she the Goddess Isis as they call her?"

Seth.Dar smiled at some memory. Perhaps he remembered the two twin girls when they danced and entertained men who had no hope of ever reaching their exalted station.

"She is at the temple near Ekur, the pyramid."

"My Misha..."

"Misha was a servant to Elanna, who could not be bothered with a child. Misha agreed to take you if we 'helped' her friend Mica to use his skills."

"I understand," she said while walking around the large empty space of the temple. She kept her distance from Seth.Dar.

"I am your father."

"Yes." *'You betrayed my mother's father and you seduced my mother.'*

Seth.Dar said nothing. He watched Celi circle him.

"So, all this time has passed. What do you want?"

"You have the rank of Counselor, rank 25. You are a granddaughter of Ningal. If she retires or dies you will be asked to serve on the Council of Twelve."

"I know this."

"In 30 days we leave aboard *Rama.* We will move hundreds to the highlands."

"Where?"

"The high plateaus in the southern continent across the western sea."

"So it will be a 'far distance' as your people like to say."

"A far distance. We will work to cultivate new crops for our land."

"And the real reason is..."

"Our fields at Eridu, Ur and Lagash are destroyed."

"What is it you do not tell me?"

"Your mate Deem is the new pilot of *Rama.*"

Celi turned away from Seth.Dar. She walked over to Harn and shyly put a hand on his arm. "Help me stand," she whispered.

She wavered, then leaned toward Harn but corrected herself and straightened her back. She began to turn toward Seth.Dar.

"Was it his choice?" she demanded.

"I do not know."

"Where is he?"

"At the Temple of Isis."

"Doing what?"

"He is trying to avoid the attention of Inanna, my half-sister, the Goddess Isis as they call her."

"You said he is 'trying to avoid' her attentions?"

"She is persuasive. She will succeed in seducing him."

There was silence for a long moment. A piece of hard wood crackled in the fire pit. *'Inanna, my mother's sister, is trying to seduce Deem?'* She felt despair for a moment, then anger. Celi looked at Seth.Dar and added, "What do you want of me?"

"I, nothing."

"You want me aboard *Rama*?"

"Yes, in 20 to 22 days."

"Will this 'Inanna' be aboard?"

"Probably. She has asked Lord Enlil to approve of her new mate."

"Does Deem know you are here?"

"No. I felt it my duty."

"Your duty?"

"To meet my daughter and offer her a better life."

"With who?" she drawled. She kept coming back to the thought of Deem in the arms of Inanna. Her mind skipped forward. '*Deem is no longer mine?*'

Seth Dar paused and saw Harn move. Harn took one step toward the older man. Seth.Dar said, "And you?" with a nod toward Harn.

"Harn has a mate. She is with their baby."

"Ah, I see. The loyal scribe."

Celi glanced at Harn and saw his face covered with dark frown. She saw also his fist, an indication of his anger.

"You want me to abandon my village, my people, for a half-possible life with a pilot who has been out of my life for what… 75 days now?"

"You must know you have the option."

"You are my father? You offer me a good life with your people?"

"Yes," he said quietly.

"You are not my father. My *real* father escaped from Eridu and is here in Arad, working on stone, his old trade. Mica will carve a stela to the people who died in Eridu.

Seth.Dar looked at her then at Harn. It was evident that Harn was Aryas, also.

"You are Aryas."

"I know this."

"You would live out your life defending these… Beag?"

Celi paused for a moment then said, "You Aryas. You are uncaring."

She looked at Seth Dar for a reaction. The man looked her in the eye without flinching. She thought, '*No conscience …have you no conscience?*'

Celi slowly chose her words. She asked Harn to remember her words. "You would allow us to be erased by an impartial force that cares nothing for the lives of our people…this shall be a banner and sign of your lives of anxious desperation."

"Yes, we struggle to save our home."

Seth.Dar looked at her then at Harn. He turned away. With his back to Celi he walked toward the main entry doors.

Celi said, "You disrespect me?"

Harn began to move to intercept the man.

"No," said Celi. "He is not worth the trouble. Leave him."

Chapter 58

The morning was quiet. The sun peeked between dark gray clouds, a pre-cursor of rain. In the cooking house two women used an open pan to scrub bowls from the morning meal. Near the river one woman was washing long sheets of fine woven cloth, purchased by Harn in Salem when he traded on of their small pistols. The other men and women were in the fields, collecting the last of the beans, radishes, and onions. The stalks of barley were now stored in the best house in Arad with the best roof.

The men worked with two short, squat animals hitched to the new Arad wagon. They were tarpon, a short semi-wild animal with a thick heavy head and yellow-brown skins. One of the tarpon had mottled brown spots on its yellow skin around both shoulders. The two animals were reluctant to pull the wagon; Harn had stated they would learn, "In two or ten days."

Dara came down in a whirlwind of dust and followed the north road until it was near the river and the Washing House. The woman at the river watched the dust cloud when it swirled over her and her wet sheets. The ramp on *Dara* came down and cloth bags were thrown onto the dusty square. An apple escaped from one bag and rolled a short distance through the dust. The bags continued to fly through the air until the pile was half the height of a man.

A man in a black tunic with a black cap came down the ramp. When he turned the woman at the river saw his badge of rank, a silver disk with straight lines radiating from the center. Many people knew this signified 'I.gi.gi' the Watchers in Space. At his waist he wore a thick leather belt that held a leather device, probably for holding a weapon. Under his tunic he wore black trousers with a white stripe sewn on the outside seam. His feet were protected in black leather attached to leather soles.

The woman at the river thought to herself, *'Straight nose, flat forehead but he looks like a possibility.'* She left her wash on the 'altar' and began to walk in his direction. The man turned and said something to a person aboard *Dara* then began to retreat away from the shuttle while its ramp closed upon itself. Two of the three engines on *Dara* began to whine and blast a stream of energy down from its vertical vents. *Dara* turned to face up the road and roared away in a storm of dust around the woman and the young officer. *Dara* flew toward Salem.

In the fields work stopped. The entire crew heard and watched *Dara* as it landed, dumped its cargo and one man, then took off. They saw the man turn to the woman and say something. They saw her point out at the fields. They saw the man try to pound the dust out of his tunic just before he began to walk in their direction.

Harn came quickly to Celi's side. He looked at the man making slow progress through the shallow river and said, "Who is he?"

Celi thought for a moment. "A high officer. They wear black."

The man climbed up the small slope from the river and began to cross the field of barley stubble. He stopped for a moment, shaded his eyes and scanned the fields and workers. Then he changed his course so he was aimed, more or less, directly at Celi. He was nearing the radish field in which she stood when she suddenly said, "He escaped."

"Escaped, my lady?"

"Yes, Harn, escaped from the clutches of a wily goddess."

"Who is it?"

"And he should not be here. I told him to stay away from Arad."

"Is it Deem?"

"Go forward. Tell him to wash himself in the Washing House. I will not receive him until I am myself ready to deal with him."

Chapter 59

In the main audience hall of the temple, Harn formed a line with his six guards. They flanked a large chair that was placed on a small platform. A small altar with a jug and two bowls stood in front of the raised platform. Off to the side four logs had been placed on the fire in a 'tent' formation; they began to flare and flame and heat the walls. When Harn felt the temple chamber was prepared, he said "Lady Celi" and she walked from the back, stepped to the platform and sat in the chair.

"Now," she said in a voice full of command.

Near the temple door the man in the black uniform had waited. He walked slowly, with what dignity he could muster, until he stood in front of the altar and looked up at Celi. His hair was washed and slicked back. He wore it cut short in the style of the Titans, those who watch.

He saw a woman radiant with sunshine. The chair was placed to receive the mid-day sun from a slit high in the roof. Her hair was lighter; it reflected glints from the sun. Her freshly washed face was darker than last he saw her. Her lips were a straight slit; she appeared formidable and capable of defending her small community. She wore the long red tunic of an Arya officer with her silver ankh mounted between her breasts.

"My lady..." he began.

"I hope the water was cold," she responded.

"My lady..." he tried.

"And you are shriveled to the size of a small round radish."

"My lady..." he tried again.

"And you were told not to come here."

"Yes, my lady."

"And yet you come?"

"I bring you as much as *Dara* could carry. Dates, figs and melons from the land of sand. Apples, grapes from the southern highlands, with a tuber, a vegetable they call 'Papa.' Oh, and a strange device with a shell you must peel, called Hor'ange. It is sweet inside."

"You expect me to be sweet inside." It was not a question.

"Why do you treat me in this manner?" he said imperiously.

"My lady!" stammered Harn with anger. He had been instructed what to do if Celi raised her left hand with one finger. He walked around the altar and kicked Deem behind the knee. Deem fell forward, almost caught himself and banged his head against the altar.

In shock almost, the pilot Deem put both hands on the altar and raised himself until he stood. His head was down. A small cut in his forehead dripped red upon the white stone of the altar. He slowly brought his eyes up to meet her frown. Her hands were now in her lap, cradling her stomach.

Celi saw a drop of blood run around his eyebrow, past his blue eyes and down his cheek until it ran off his chin. Her stomach churned. She motioned with her hand and Harn moved away; he returned to stand just behind her.

Deem nodded in the direction of her swollen stomach.

"My lady," began Deem slowly, "Is this why?"

She saw that he glanced at Harn and said, "Harn is my most trusted advisor. He was there when the Black Death roiled up the canyon and past our cave. He was there when our guard died. He was here when Arad held piles of black poison."

"My lady," Deem tried to say.

"And you were not," she added.

Deem stood. His head dropped; he stared at the jug and the bowls on the altar.

"Some who visit us are welcome. We share from a common jug."

Harn began to walk toward the altar.

"But you are not."

Harn stopped in confusion. He had not seen Celi act this way with other guests. Especially with a man who brought bags upon bags of fruit to help their small village.

"Yes, my lady," said Deem and he raised his eyes to hers. He saw, he believed, a drop of water in the corner of one eye.

"Who are you? For the record. Our scribe will record your visit."

"Deem, Captain of the *Rama,*" he began and then added "great-grandson of our Lord Enlil."

"And I am Celi, Mistress of Arad, granddaughter of Ningal who sits on the Council of Twelve and approves decisions made by your *high lord called Enlil*."

Deem seemed confused. He did not know the protocol.

"I am not a goddess," she added. Harn launched into a smile.

Deem saw the smile in the corners of Harn's lips and frowned. "Your advisor insults me," he warned.

"And you would do what? Drop a weapon on us? Destroy us?"

"No, my lady."

"Deem, I trusted you. In fact, I believe I loved you."

"The decision to launch the weapons, to destroy the restricted zone, was made by the Council."

"We are not loyal to Enlil, or to Enki, great as they may be. Nor are we loyal to a pilot who intends to direct the *Rama* to the southern continent then the long flight to Nibiru.

"My role, if I choose it," he remarked.

"You wear the uniform," she countered.

"I do. I can go anywhere. My rank gives me privilege."

"Except in Arad."

He looked up at her face. She did not smile. It was clear she was not warming to his style and bravado.

"When do you leave?" she asked.

Off to her side there was an intake of breath. She glanced at Harn and saw he was clearly upset by her question.

Deem's head dropped. He looked at two bowls on the altar and picked up one.

"I have not decided," he began.

"Then decide," remarked Celi with grim finality.

"Ten days," he said.

He looked up at her face. She seemed grim. He began to hiccup and smiled. He knew the hiccups came on whenever he was in a difficult situation. He smiled and she stared at him. To his mate Celi, his smile *seemed prophetic*. She instantly knew he would leave in ten days.

Chapter 60

Celi declared a day of rest. The last of the radishes and onions were out of the fields. The wheat had been harvested and waited to be sifted and ground into flour. The second crops of beans, lentils, and a new item, black beans had sprouted and were one hand tall. The small field of 'Papa' had grown well but Eglan, the field leader, was unsure when they should dig up the round, hard shells.

In Arad the houses around the temple had new roofs. Many had been white washed. The women saw the crew of three who did the painting; their faces and clothes were white. They became known as the 'white-wall' crew.

The shadow of the western mountains was crawling across the valley when Celi and Harn, her advisor now, walked out to the grove. They found a red granite slab, partially carved. "It required four strong men to get that slab from 'our' mountain valley to here," remarked Harn.

Celi smiled. It was a notable project. She had planned to get the memorial finished sometime in the near future. The need for the steps out of the washing pool became a priority and Mica now had two men working with him. She looked at the old gnarled trees of the grove and said, "We must replace these old trees with young trees ...palm trees, I believe."

She looked in the direction of the washing house and saw Lara walking toward the old grove. "I think Lara wants to tell us something."

"How do you know?" asked Harn.

"Your mate, Gran. She saw Lara smile at my Mica."

As Lara approached Celi said, "You are smiling."

"Yes, my lady. I bring a good question, I think."

Harn smiled and began to walk away. Celi stopped him with, "You may ask in front of Harn."

"That house by the river, where Mica is cutting stone. He works hard. He is a gentle man. We want to live there."

"You are asking my permission?"

"We talk. He is quiet. We have come to like each other."

Celi looked at Harn and winked. She smiled at Lara and said, "You think it is proper to join with my grandfather?"

"He is strong. He is gentle. We will take care of each other."

"Lara ...you have my permission although it is hardly needed. You both live here in Arad. Harn and I and the others will be happy for you."

Lara bowed toward her lady, out of respect. She turned to walk toward the shore where Mica worked. As she left, Lady Celi thought, *she has had enough of sadness. Abused by Char; then he died.*

The next day as the sun touched the western mountains Lara and Mica came to the plaza. All the people of Arad attended their ceremony. They pledged to share forever their water and their smiles for each other. Two of the guards brought jugs of fermented barley and the people pledged their support.

Many of the women were immensely pleased that Lara had a man to share her life with. Celi was happy for Mica. He had been without his Misha for a long time. She saw him cough once. He wiped his lips with his hand and came away with a touch of blood on his hand.

Chapter 61

Sparse white clouds strung out over the canvas blue. Three women and a man were walking up the path toward the trail into 'their' mountain. Behind them they left a wagon and two tarpon. Deem, dressed in work clothes and gloves had tethered the two tarpon where an old road crossed the river. It was a warm day; the two beasts were thirsty. Celi was spreading an old blanket across the grass of the river bank. She sat on the blanket and pulled a small bag toward her. From the bag she took a bowl of grapes. Then she spread her long red coat across the blanket so it would not wrinkle. She pulled her straw hat down over her eyes; the mid-day sun made her squint.

She leaned back to her right and put her elbow on the blanket. She watched Deem retying the ropes at the feet of the tarpon. One of them sniggered and almost stepped on his hand. He stood up and looked at Celi. She waved to tell him to use the other half of the blanket. He came, sat down then stretched out to look at the clouds.

"Wind blows from the East," she said. Celi remembered the evil black cloud that came from the east and brought death to four members of her small village.

"But then a strong wind came from over the mountains and down the canyon and scrubbed this tree and other trees in its path and blew away the Black Poison that scarred our country."

Deem did not react. He felt uncertain of his role in her world. They had come to the canyon mouth with a small party to retrieve jugs and blankets and other items left behind in the rush to vacate the cave. Celi had placed him in charge of the two tarpon that were hitched to the wagon. When their crew left for the cave, she stayed behind with him.

"You have worked these five days without complaint."

"Yes, my lady."

"And your shoulders have turned the red of sunset."

"Long time at the helm of *Dara* then *Cead,*" he said as explanation.

"Why did you come?"

"Here? You told me to…"

"No, back to Arad. Why did you come?"

Deem studied the water in the river where it meandered past their tree. The water was clear with a dark brown sheen on the rocks of the bottom. An occasional leaf floated by their spot on the bank. Celi reclined quietly on the blanket.

Deem picked up a stone and tossed it toward the stream. He was in the act of throwing a second stone when she said, "Why?"

He looked over at her and saw her eyes and the mid-day light behind her pale brown hair. "My mate lives in Arad."

"And?"

"It seemed my duty."

"Your duty?"

"Yes, to see if my mate was still my mate, my companion from our days spent together in Arad. Days we spent talking about the future."

"Why did you doubt your mate?" she hesitated with fear.

"You sent a message not to come back to Arad."

Deem sat up and braced himself with his hands. He looked at Celi.

"Ah, yes. I meant what I said."

He looked down at his knee and flicked off a small bug. He brought his knee up and wrapped his arms around his leg before putting his head on his leg. Without looking he added, "I was greatly sad from your message."

She said nothing. "Why sad?"

"I believed, all this time, bringing royals here and there, helping them escape the Black Cloud, that in Arad I had a mate who was loyal and determined and waiting for my return."

He turned his head away from her. There was silence. He waited. He felt, at that moment, that if he looked he might begin to shed tears.

"It has been three moons," she said. "You performed for others."

"Three moons?"

"That long, yes." She wanted to tell him about her meeting with her father Seth.Dar and his assertion that she could join the *Rama* and her mate.

"You and the Goddess Isis can have the *Rama.*"

"What is this?"

"I know all about the lovely Goddess. I saw her once, she of the long legs and curled hair and flowing gowns, she and her maidens and their wiles and wine and songs and padded sleeping platforms."

"What do you know?"

"Her name is Inanna." *'I will not tell you she is my mother's sister.'*

"What did you hear?"

"She decided to capture your soul, we heard."

Deem took a long breath and turned his head toward Celi. He could hardly believe she would listen to stories about the 'handsome pilot' and his lady at the Temple of Isis. What she and all others did not know was that the Goddess Isis asked him once. His response had been an emphatic rejection of her entreaty. *'Capture my soul?'*

'What do I say?' he thought.

"Once, just once," began Deem, "There was a time I knew you for a '*demon*' who captured my soul."

"A demon?"

"A beautiful demon in a dream. Was it not real?" he began but added, "There was once I think... my beautiful demon loves me."

"And now?"

"I do not know."

"You know that we will have a baby?"

"Yes. I am glad. Even to the edge of exploding with joy."

"You are happy that I have your baby?"

"Who could not be happy?"

"Why? Tell me why?" she asked.

"The baby is ours. Yours and mine. We created this baby."

Celi turned back to look at him. She reached out to touch his arm. He felt her hand and jumped. She frowned at his reaction but said, "Can you help us to gather the joy and memories we first felt when we were together?"

"What do you ask me? Your words? They confuse me."

"In your mind, in your memories, am I still *'your'* spirit?" She remembered the first time and her joining with him to make a baby. *'I wanted a baby. You were convenient. I know I loved you.'* She smiled at the thought.

Deem turned to look at the stream. A small log floated by. There was a flash of light in the water. A small fish swam to the surface and grabbed a fly. He knew his words might determine their future. With slow reluctance he began "I do not know..."

Celi felt more than saw his confusion.

"If you do not know, then you do not belong to me and our baby."

Chapter 62

Their crew of women with one guard returned from the canyon. They brought three empty water jugs and old blankets. They also brought a copper bowl. Celi remembered the women using the bowl to make stew in their long twelve days in the cave. She could not believe it was left behind.

"But then, we did not think about food."

"Was this when…?"

"When we moved from the cave back to Arad," she finished.

Celi and Deem watched the women and the guard pile what they brought into the old wagon. Their small 'horses' the tarpon were anxious; they wanted to move. Harn had finally given up on riding them. He declared they would be pulling beasts, only.

"My lady?" said the guard.

Celi turned to look at him and the women.

"Should we gather the clothes that were left behind?"

She looked around the camp. There were three piles of clothes, left behind when the women made the last dash to the cave. The four wagons stood where they were left on the day of the Black Cloud. The bloated carcasses of the horses littered the ground near the trees. One of their stomachs had exploded; black flies filled the air.

'What a waste?' she thought.

"We reap the harvest of our lords and their wars."

"No," she said to the guard. "We will burn everything. But not today."

She watched as the guard helped the three women climb into the wagon. One of them smacked him lightly when he forgot and put his hand on her hip. But she smiled afterward. Celi smiled. They are mates, she explained to Deem.

The guard motioned towards Celi; he wanted to help her into the wagon. She waved him off. She meant to walk. The guard moved to the head of the nearest tarpon and placed his hand on the leather harness that ran through the tarpon's mouth. He pulled and the tarpon objected. The small 'horse' raised his head. The guard pulled down hard and the tarpon lowered his head. The two tarpon began to pull the wagon.

Celi and Deem followed. She allowed the wagon to get ahead before she said to Deem,

"You do not know if you love me?"

Deem glanced at her and turned his head to watch the wagon ahead of him.

"I am so tired," mumbled Deem.

Should I tell her I met Seth Dar? he pondered. *He almost declared the 'princess Celiste' would join his people to rebuild villages in the highlands.*

"Tired of these royals and their demands. They ask for much. They do nothing for the people who serve them."

"I see..." she answered.

"Do you?"

"I have been aware of their arrogance," she answered, "...their power and their disdain for the brown-haired Beag since I met a Vizier in Salem who whipped a servant girl for touching my robe."

"Is he still alive?"

"Yes," she laughed. She began to bend over to pick up a large copper comb from the side of the trail. Deem reached over and stopped her.

"It contains the evil that kills."

She straightened up and thought about his words.

They walked on, quietly.

After a long silence Celi finally asked him again, "Do you think you love me?"

Deem was silent.

They walked on. Ahead the wagon slowly moved through a shallow stream. Deem waited until the wagon was farther ahead and said, "Would my lady allow me to lift her across the stream?"

Celi looked at him and said, "No. You do not touch me until you know."

"Know if I love you?"

"How many ways must I say it?" she responded. She pulled her white work trousers up on her calves, knowing they would get wet. Then she proceeded to walk across the shallow stream. She looked back at Deem on the other shore.

"Are you going to join us?"

He smiled and said, "My choice. That is my choice. To join you?"

She turned away from him and resumed her walking after the wagon.

'She gives me a choice,' he thought.

He watched her back and her hips as she walked after the wagon.

"You want me to say, 'I love you' and live in Arad?"

She was too far away and did not hear his words.

Chapter 63

On the third day after their joining Lara reported that Mica spit up blood twice. He remarked his stomach hurt. He felt weak in the early morning, but stronger in the afternoon. Lara reported he was building steps on the bank of the river, slowly. The steps were to help her, or any of the people, to step down to the river to retrieve water.

When Celi asked about his pain and the blood, Lara noted he had shown symptoms for about one moon. "He continues to say 'It is nothing'." When Celi did not respond Lara added, "I am afraid the pain is from the Black Dust or maybe from the stones he works on."

"After our baby comes I will travel to Salem and seek healing advice from Lady Nin.ĝar.Sag who directs the Place of Healing."

"Lara, I hope you realize how fortunate you are."

"My lady?"

Celi smiled at Lara and at Eglan and Gran who stood nearby. "She said, 'our baby'."

Black clouds roiled up over the western mountains and spread their pallor over Arad and the valley that stretched to the White Sea. A few drops of rain fell; the rain god laughed at those who hoped for more rain on their fields. Rain on this side of the mountains had been slight. The river that served Arad was low and Eglan declared it was time to clean the canals. She led a large crew this day: three of the men and twelve women. They carried digging sticks and pots to scoop mud from the small canals. Several women greeted Mica as they passed him.

The point where Mica chose to build his steps was a shallow place; rounded river stones guarded the river. If a person with a pot chose to they could step into the river to gather water.

Near the river Mica sat on a box and studied his steps. His two helpers were absent, sent by Lady Celi to burn everything at their 'camp' near the mountains. When Lara asked him if he was going to work he said, "One last step, by the water."

She watched him for a short time then walked over to the washing house to begin washing and hanging towels from the previous day.

Mica began to place the support rocks, small hand sized rocks that would support the larger rock step. He pushed the small rocks down into the mud and added a second layer of rocks, then a third layer. When he was satisfied he could no longer add the small rocks he looked at the large one-piece rock that would be the step at water level. He had chosen this rock for its size; a person could stand easily on this step and fill their containers.

"Too large," he said, and smiled at himself.

He stepped out of the river and up the steps. At the rock he lifted it slowly and flopped it over onto a rope. Then he flopped it over a second time so there were two strands of rope under the rock. When he straightened up he felt dizzy. His world swirled around him for a moment. Then he shook his head, grabbed the rope and began to slide the rock to the river edge. The rock reached the small slope to the river and began to slide. Mica walked backward into the river, pulling the rock down the slope. The rock reached the river edge; Mica stopped.

In his mind Mica saw himself lifting the rock and placing it on the support rocks. He knew he was strong enough; he felt challenged. *Good to finish it,* he thought.

He squatted down and spread his arms to each end of the rock. He grabbed hold of the rock and began to lift. Then he straightened his legs and pulled. The rock resisted his pull. *The mud sucks the rock,* he thought. Then the rock came out of the mud and he lifted. The rock was almost to his waist when he felt his left foot slide. He began to move his load toward the steps and felt himself falling backward. He continued to lift the rock, but to no effect. The rock pushed him over; he fell backward and his head came down hard on a smooth river rock.

He realized he was in the river; a puzzled look of surprise crossed his face. His eyes closed. His head slowly slipped off the rock and into the water.

In the Washing House his mate Lara glanced out the window that faced their house with its bright white paint. When she did not see him she concluded he had gone in to rest.

Eglan entered the Washing House. She saw Lara and began to walk toward her. What Lara saw was Eglan's normally smiling face; her lips were curled down in sadness. Lara looked out the window toward her house and saw four women pulling Mica out of the river.

"No!" she screamed. "No! Not my Mica?"

Eglan held her by her shoulders for a moment. Lara looked into Eglan's eyes and saw tears. Eglan wrapped her arms around Lara and pulled her close. Quietly, Lara began to cry.

"Mica was underwater when I found him. His spirit has fled, gone into the sky to join those who went before us."

Lara raised her head and looked at the tear that crawled down Eglan's face. "No?" she asked. "It is not Mica. It is someone else?"

"It is Mica," whispered Eglan, afraid to say the words. "We will wash him and wrap him then I will take you to him."

Chapter 64

Four men were at work before the sun rose. They went to the old clutch of trees on the western edge of Arad and began to dig. They hit rock at a depth of two cubits and were forced to stop. Celi appeared and inspected the burial hole. "Mica will rest here. He will watch the sun on its long path to Osiris." She turned and walked toward Lara's house.

The sky in the east began to lighten. Time passed before bright yellow sunlight flared across the valley and lit the White Sea and the village of Arad. The sun touched the eastern mountains as it rose. From the house of Mica and Lara came a small procession. Six men walked slowly with a wrapped bundle suspended between them. Behind them came Lara, Lady Celi, Gran and Eglan. Lara wore a dark red cloth over her head; she was afraid to see the day. The other three women wore dark red shawls.

They proceeded to the grove of old trees where the village waited. The body of Mica was placed on top of three ropes. The six men lifted him and gently lowered him into the ground.

There were long moments of silence. The women near Lara could see her eyes were red.

"We have lost..." began Lady Celi, "...a good man, a man we could not afford to lose."

"We have lost..." added Eglan, "...a man who came to us from Eridu."

"We have lost..." added Gran, "...a man who worked in stone."

It was the traditional start of the ceremony. Three friends would tell the community what it had lost before the mate, in this case, added her thoughts.

"He was a man of stone," said Lara. "We worked together. He was gentle, and calm, and trusting. I have lost my Mica."

The old woman who directed the Washing House brought a deep red flower to Lara. It was the flower of mourning that grew near the river. Lara took the flower and dropped it onto the body of Mica. She stood near his grave for a long time. Someone stepped up to her side and whispered in her ear. She nodded and turned away. Her friend Gran walked her back to her house where she would spend the day in thoughts of Mica.

"We have lost..." began Celi. She felt a little queasy. She looked up at Deem where he stood at the outside of the gathering. He stared back at her. She did not move. A stone turned in her stomach. *To lose Mica. And tomorrow is the tenth day. How can I carry this pain?* Her friend Gran, standing next to her, touched her elbow.

"We have lost my Mica. He was my Mica. He was my father when I was young. We worked together on Lord Enki's temple. He was fond of saying 'Look, always look to go forward' That must be our rule, if such be a rule, here in Arad." Her head dipped. Her shoulders heaved. She began to turn and staggered. Gran grabbed her and helped her walk away from the grove.

Chapter 65

On the tenth day Deem did not come to the morning meal. Harn, to no one in particular reported that the captain was dressing himself in his uniform and boots. Heads around the table drooped. The women knew a few details about Celi's treatment of the young captain, but wondered why she would send him away.

Celi entered the dining hall wearing her usual work clothes, a short tunic across the curve of her stomach with gray cloth leggings. Her hair was bound in a red rag that held her hair tight to her head. In one hand she held several cloth bags; the bags would hold produce from the field. Her other hand held a digging stick used to chop plants.

She stopped near the end of the long table and looked across her friends and her fellow workers. Harn raised himself off his bench and indicated a spot for Celi to sit. She waved him off.

"Today we finish the melons. They cannot last longer in the field."

There were two or three groans from among the workers. Lara stood up and waved an arm to indicate the women.

"Eglan and Gran both say the melons will be ripe…" began Celi before Lara held up a hand with a fist.

"This is not a Council meeting to decide," said Celi. A flash memory of her grandfather telling his men not to argue with his decisions crossed her mind.

"I want to say something," said Lara.

"About melons?"

"No, about my situation."

Celi looked at Harn, then Gran, then the rest of the gathered women. They were all looking at Lara. Some dropped their faces to the table, in sadness.

"Go ahead, Lara," she said but added needlessly, "Lara may talk."

"You asked, some days ago, whether I was happy."

Celi's face became blank and then began to frown.

"These past days, with a man to share my house?" After a moment she added, "Yes."

Harn stood up and raised a hand. Lara ignored him.

"Those of us who have no mates," she added then paused. *'Should I say this to my friend? Our mistress?'*

"...wonder if you realize what you are doing. Your man has worked for nine days elbow to elbow with all of us. He says words to describe you that any of us would collapse on the ground and cry to hear said by a man."

"This is not your place," said Celi.

Harn raised his hand and said, "Drop your hand."

"I am not improper," stated Lara. "This question relates to all of us here, those with mates and those without mates."

Celi's face began to show a smidgen of deep red in her cheeks. She looked around the women and the two guards who sat near the end of the long table and said, "This is our village."

"Which means what?"

"We can be proud in what we have done. Rebuilt fifteen of the houses, raised crops, birthed two babies with two on the way. And I shall not be silent about this ...none of you are slaves. You are my sisters. We will build our village into a safe place for children and families. We will ignore the animosity between the royals, those Lords who fashion themselves to be gods."

Gran stood up. The color seemed to rise in her cheeks.

"I know," said Celi. "I am Aryas ...I am royal, as are you Gran." She stopped for a long moment then added, "I should not admit this to you."

"Then do not," said Harn.

"But I must."

She looked across her squad of thirty women. "There was a time when I believed the Beag, you in front of me, were worth less than an Aryas."

"But I have watched you with our two babies, how you care for them. In a way, I am jealous. All of you want to be mothers."

Lara raised her hand with a fist. When the murmuring of the women died down, she said,

"And yet you would cast away your young man, because he shared his attentions on a vain and seductive woman?"

"He had no chance, at all, a'tall," said a woman.

Laughter erupted. It was a form of release. Several women tapped the table top with their bowls, signifying agreement.

Chapter 66

A guard posted near the entrance to the temple, entered the cooking house and walked over to Harn. He said something quietly into Harn's ear and Harn nodded at Celi. She took it to mean the shuttle was on the ground, her mate would be leaving.

Outside, she saw the *Dara* was once again at the end of the road by the Washing House. It was turned so the ramp faced Celi's temple. A cloud of dust was slowly dissipating from a slow breeze from the west. Deem was not in sight.

Celi waited, confused. She turned to look in the direction of the men's house and saw him stepping out from the doorway. *"Time to get paint on that house,"* she thought in distraction. She watched him approach. He looked regal in his black uniform with the black cap. He wore a colored ribbon around his neck that held a copper and gold medallion.

When he stopped in front of her, she blurted "that is beyond belief." She nodded toward his medallion.

"Yes, I suppose. Awarded by Enlil, our master. For my three 'moons,' as you call them, service to the royal family."

"Four moons," she blurted.

He ignored her comment and said, "I am leaving."

"It is your choice," she said. *'Is it my choice?'* she asked herself. She felt a mote of dust in her eye and rubbed at it.

"It was your decision," he added. He reached up to flick a large nodule of dirt off her cheek and said, "*Dara* kicks up a cloud of dirt."

Her hand came up and grabbed his hand. To herself she said, *'You are still my best friend, from years past.'* Deem looked into her eyes and saw his face reflected in the water that welled up in her eyes. He rested his hand on her cheek then bent over to kiss her lightly on the other cheek.

He straightened up.

"You do not love me?" she asked. *'You do not know if you love me?'*

He looked at her, turned away and walked toward the shuttle. The ramp lowered to admit him as he approached. He put one foot on the ramp and stopped. He stood without moving. She watched him.

Far above, in the clear sky, she heard a hawk make a cry. *'Asking for her mate?'* she thought. A crew man appeared at the top of *Dara's* ramp. She could not hear what they said to each other.

His cap came off his head. He grabbed it and threw it into the shuttle. She saw him reach to his neck to remove the medallion and ribbon, which he also threw into the shuttle. By this time the engines on the shuttle were beginning to blast at the ground. A cloud of dust rose from underneath the shuttle. He disappeared. When she saw him his black officer's tunic was gone; the shuttle rose out of the flying dust behind him.

He walked directly back to her and stopped. He looked into her eyes. She looked amazed at his actions. "I do know. If you do not yourself know, then I will serve your village of Arad for as long as I am able." He paused. "To be near you..." he added. She tried to put two of her fingers across his lips but he took her hand in his.

"We have a saying, among the pilots and shuttle crews. 'Sand builds hills.' You will build this village, and its fields. I know, my love."

"Are you confident?"

"That I know?" he said. An eyebrow rose.

"No, you are a stubborn man," she remarked. She looked at Deem for a long minute before she added, "That last part. You said, 'My love'."

He smiled and nodded, "This is our Shin'ar, my love."

'My love,' she said to herself. Aloud she said, "Your words are music."

Chapter 67

The sun broke across the distant mountains. A heron flew across the sleepy village of Arad on its path toward the eastern sea. A guard, standing lonely vigil in the early morning, watched the heron and said aloud, "You will not like it. It tastes of salt."

In the cooking house one of the women stirred herself, rubbed an eye and added kindling to the embers of the cook fire. In the washing house the oldest of Celi's women began her daily task of bringing water from the river. The guard by the temple scanned the area then walked toward the men's house to nudge his relief out of his slumber.

When he entered the men's house someone in the gray light said, "Where is the pilot?"

Someone else said, "Where he belongs. Now stop your chatter."

In the sleeping chambers of Lady Celi, all was quiet. The encroaching light from the east showed the lady herself, stretched out on her sleeping platform next to her mate. He was asleep on his back with her blanket on his chest and one hand under his head.

She waved a flying distraction away from his face. He must have sensed her action because he suddenly said, "There is one thing. We must get rid of this blanket."

"You do not like onions?" she laughed.

His nose crinkled. He smiled with his eyes closed.

EPILOG

(THE AUTHOR'S FOOTNOTE)

Shin'ar My Love tells the story of Celiste, daughter of Dea, granddaughter of Ningal, fifth generation after Enoch, the builder of the Great Pyramid. Celi is a royal (Anunnaki) princess who is asked to guide/direct a squad of women while they rebuild a village in southern Israel. *This novel* is historical fiction; it is an attempt to popularize the story of the Anunnaki Lords and their guidance of the new race: *Homo Sapiens.*

The pre-history of Sumeria and Egypt was in the background; the foreground held the story of Celiste and Deem, two members of the Aryan race who faced challenges during the war of 2024 BCE. This is Celi's story.

This war, with its devastating destruction of nine cities actually happened and is recorded in the Sumerian tablets, copies of which were found in the library of King Ashurbanipal at Nineveh. This was the period when the Third Dynasty of Ur rose to pre-eminence and cultural influence and then fell into decline in the period 2124 to 2024 BC. Ur was the home-village of Abram (AB.RAM in Sumerian; Abram in Akkadian).

Abram and his family left Ur and went to Harran. At the age of 70 Abram led a 'cavalry' of 100 camel-mounted warriors in the War of the Kings. AB.RAM was a member of the family Ib.Ri (in Sumerian; the term later becomes 'Hebrew').

The land of Shin'ar (aka Sumer) became an arena for contending loyalties and opposing armies in the period 2100 BC to 2000 BC. A large number of culturally strong centers (Indus Valley in NW India and the Akkad-Sumer Empire) suffered a major cataclysm. In the Indus Valley the power centers of the Hittite Kings (Mohenjo-Daro and Harappa) were attacked with nuclear weapons. Sodom and Gomorrah and Zoar in today's Israel were destroyed.

Historian Zacharia Sitchen proposed a blast of seven nuclear missiles (called Brilliance of ӾEnlil) hit southern Israel and the Sinai in 2024 BC and the radioactive cloud devastated the seven southern cities in Sumeria. Those seven cities were Eridu (Enki's Temple), Ur (called EN.LIL.KI, place of Enlil), Erech (Anu's City), Larsa, Lagash, Nippur (the Command Center) and Babylon. The nuclear blasts (in Israel) were for the purpose of destroying 'wicked cities.' The radioactive cloud that destroyed seven cities was an unforeseen accident. In the aftermath, the people and their animals and plants were killed. It required 70 years before these cities were again declared habitable.

ӾEnlil, the Sumerian name for 'Lord of the Land' became Elohim in the Hebrew Scriptures, according to Josephus

There is, however, no record yet located of *when* Mohenjo-Daro and Harappa, in the Hittite Empire were destroyed by Rama, unless a reader interprets the war described in the *Mahabharata* and *Ramayana,* epic historical poems of India. (Side Note: Mar.Duk fled from Babylon to western India. He adopted the name Rama, built Dwarka and in an act of vengeance against the Hittite kings destroyed Mohenjo Daro and Harappa. His capital city has been found at a depth of 250 feet, west of the current city of Dwarka.)

WHY THIS NOVEL?

In the western world so little is known about the history of the world before Sumeria and the Great Flood. A technological civilization existed and built the Sphinx, the Great Pyramid, Tiwanaku in Bolivia, New Grange in Ireland, Cuzco and Macchu Pichu in Peru and brought law, mathematics and astronomy to early cultures. Recent research suggests the Great Pyramid was a producer of microwave energy used to fuel Anunnaki ships 'on station' above Egypt. The engineer Christopher Dunn believes diluted hydrochloric acid and hydrated zinc were sent down the shafts into the Queen's chamber to produce hydrogen gas as an energy source for the resonating chamber (the King's Chamber).

Comets and asteroids have 'attacked' Earth. Did the Vela Supernova debris cause the end of the Ice Age? Did a comet cause devastation in 9,600 BC? Did an attack of seven 'flaming swords' in 7640 B.C. result in craters off the coast of South Carolina (USA) and the opening of the Bosporus Strait to flood the Black Sea? Did a later comet/asteroid attack (2,807 B.C.) cause the Great Flood of Noah?

There is a theory that Mars was devastated, destroyed by an enormous comet or asteroid attack. The attack created the Tharsis Bulge and opened up the 2,000-mile gorge, *Valles Marineris*. There is an alternative theory that a passing planet sent a 'thunderbolt' of electrical energy that 'carved' the *Valles Marineris*.

Velikovsky's ground-breaking work *Worlds in Collision* suggests a bright, burning star visited Earth at the time of the Exodus (–1450 BC) from Egypt and turned our world over four times in six days. The sun set in the East, then the West, the East then the West. This close encounter also produced enormous thunderbolts from the star into the Earth. The star became Venus. (Part II, Chapter 3). Or, is there a brown dwarf star traveling with Nibiru (Planet X) as it approaches Earth?

Could such a close pass from Mars have created the enormous gorge known as the *Valles Marineris*? In 747 BC a series of by-passes with Mars began. Mars continued to revolve in 'near-earth' orbit until 687 to 669 BC. A thunderbolt discharge created Lake Bolsema (Italy). During this century the length of the year was revised several times. After 669 BC the Earth assumed her orbit and time of rotation of 365.25 days. In 747 BC the Earth's rotation was 360 days. (Velikovski Part II, Chapter 8).

The evacuation of Mars, and abandonment of the 'city' of pyramids on the Cydonia plain occurred before the comet/asteroid hit Mars. Zacharia Sitchen hinted the Anunnaki lords had a 'way-station' on Mars to which gold ingots were transferred to be loaded on large 'Deep Black' vessels for shipment to Nibiru. (That will remain conjecture until Earth's astronauts actually visit the ruins of buildings on Mars). There is conjecture that the moon Phobos is/was an arcology. One picture of Phobos shows what could be an exhaust vent for a rocket engine. 'Phobos II,' a Russian mission was somehow destroyed while photographing Phobos. A recent release from the 'Russian Space Agency' (ie. 2010) shows a light streak coming from Phobos toward their mission. Was it a missile? Or possibly a laser weapon?

What of more recent attacks? In 1178 AD a comet/asteroid estimated at two kilometers in diameter hit the moon with a force of 100,000 megatons of TNT. Current nuclear weapons are rated at 50 megatons. The crater was seen when astronauts flew around the Moon.

In 2028 an asteroid 1997 XF11 with a diameter of almost two kilometers may pass or collide with the Earth. A collision would destroy much of our planet.

In 2126 comet Swift-Tuttle will return on its 134-year cycle. If it reaches perihelion with the Sun on 26 July 2126 it will collide with the Earth. Current research predicts perihelion on 19 July 2126. (True, that warning is off in the distant future).

There are reports that a small asteroid, 30 kilometers across, broke off a much larger body. They are both inside the Taurus 'doughnut' through which the Earth passes twice each year. Is it possible the 'much larger mass' is a remnant of the planet Nibiru? And when will that 'larger mass' become a threat to the Earth?

Ukranian astronomers (in 2013) received credit for locating a 400-meter asteroid with a dangerous trajectory. They have projected a potential collision with earth on August 26, 2032. They also said the odds of an impact are 1 in 63,000. Did Mayan astronomers predict this event? If Spanish priests were off by one Ka'tun, the end of the last 'Mayan' age will occur on 7 September 2032.

Your task is to learn the ancient history of our planet. Your immediate task is to ask why the leaders of our troubled Earth are doing so little to prepare for an asteroid or comet attack.

The Need to Hold an Open Mind:

When we look to the past to 'divine' and understand mankind's history, we look through the distorting lens of the present.

The Need to Prepare:
We of Earth suffer from collective amnesia. We have forgotten the disasters that destroyed earlier civilizations and wiped their memory from our minds. We have forgotten the nuclear war of 2024 B.C. and we have ignored the causes of the two great floods in our pre-history. The pyramids that were hit with a massive blast on the Cydonia plain of Mars are a reminder that our Earth could be hit by a cataclysm of cosmic proportions. We must prepare, and not just put words to the need to prepare but hold our leaders responsible for not preparing.

(Dr. F. Martin Duncan, 2016)

END NOTES

End Note 1: The first of the twelve Anunnaki (those whose father was Anu) was an engineer named Ea. His name meant, 'He who makes the water move.' His purpose was to reclaim gold from seawater. He landed at the delta of the four rivers at the head of the Persian Gulf. Here he built what would become the first city of the delta, Eridu, his blessed city.

'Four rivers:' the four rivers were the Pishon, from Arabia, the Gihon from the mountains in the northeast, and the Tigris and Euphrates rivers which flowed southeast past Nippur and Eridu to the Persian Gulf.

Ea built canals to force seawater past his concentrators. He quickly discovered there were only trace elements of gold in the seawater. He sent a message to Anu and the Twelve arrived and began the search for sources of gold. Nibiru, the home planet, needed to disperse atomized gold into its atmosphere, to increase the reflectivity of its upper atmosphere.

Ea became known as ✕Enki, Lord of the Waters.

End Note 2: The Council of Twelve held ultimate control over Ki.En (Earth). They were six men and their wives. King Anu held the rank of 60; his wife held the rank of 55. Lord Enlil held rank of 50; his half-brother Enki (Ea) held rank 40. The spouse of Nan.Nar (aka Sin) was Ningal, rank 25. For the purpose of this novel she is the grandmother of Celiste, who will achieve rank 25 when she reaches the age of 20 years.

End Note 3: The Beag ('short' in Gaelic) are the children of our human ancestors, the Adamu (which meant 'first man'). They were created from *Homo Habilis* in a 'Special Event' approximately 50 to 40 thousand years ago, to be slaves in the mines.

End Note 4: 'The mines' called Abzu were built in what is now South Africa. They were also known as 'Punt' by the Egyptians. The Adamu labored through many generations to dig for gold ore that was taken to Bad Tibura (northeast of Eridu) to be smelted. A recent suggestion from South American archeologists suggests Tiwanaku (in Bolivia) was an ore processing site.

End Note 5: Ur, the sacred city southeast of Eridu, rose to prominence and cultural influence then fell into decline in the period 2124 BC to 2024 BC. During this period Abram, 'father' of the Hebrews led his family away from Ur and became leader of Enlil's army in the West. This era ended with a nuclear war of devastating consequences.

End Note 6: *Dara* is a shuttle used for flights from Earth to heavier vehicles in space. The Indian chronicles describe a *Vimana* as a vertical vehicle that lands on its propulsion system. In this novel the shuttle has short, stubby wings that allow it to maneuver in the atmosphere.

End Note 7: The sixth planet, as you enter the solar system, is Mars. The planet is represented by the six pointed star. The seventh planet is Earth, usually represented by a larger dot near a smaller dot: the Moon. Or perhaps represented by a circle with seven gems. On the Sumerian cylinder seal called 'Granting of the Plow' the entire Solar System is portrayed, including the outer three planets that were not discovered until the 19th century.

End Note 8: Salem, also called 'Shalem,' was the Radiant Place; also called Ur-Shulim, which meant 'City of Shulim' to the Sumerian scribes, was the 'Supreme Place of the Four Regions.' It was also the Mission Control Center northwest of the Dead Sea. It is today called Jerusalem.

End Note 9: The 'Temple Mount' in Jerusalem, with its enormous stone monoliths, was a landing pad for heavy vehicles, similar to Baalbek in Lebanon or (perhaps) Saksaywaman outside Cuzco or Ollantaytambo (both in Peru).

End Note 10: The 'White Sea' is also called the Sea of Death, or Dead Sea. It is a source of salt for the entire region. The village of Arad is to the west of the Dead Sea. The villages of Sodom, Gomorrah and Zoar were located to the south of the Dead Sea.

End Note 11: The 'highlands' in the southern continent were in Bolivia. After the Great Deluge survivors (possibly from Atlantis) came to the high lands to begin agricultural work to perfect strains of maize, wheat, barley and radishes). The remnants of their field irrigation system near Lake Titicaca are visible from space. Other survivors began field crops in Anatolia region, Turkey on the higher elevations near the site of Gobekli Tepe

End Note 12: The 'Titans' ('Those who Watch from Space') were called I.gi.gi (in Sumerian) and were proud of their role of maintenance of the space vehicles. They were the Sons of Gods who came down and mated with the Daughters of Earth.

End Note 13: 'Rules for Succession:' In the ancient cuneiform tablets unearthed in Shin'ar (Sumeria) in Eridu and Nippur and Nineveh, the scribes describe the rules for succession among the Anunnaki. Enki ('EA' in Akkadian) arrived to mine gold from sea-water in the delta called E.Din in Sumerian texts. His half-brother Enlil was the legal successor of ӾAnu, king of Nibiru ('Crossing' in Sumerian). Enlil's father was Anu and his mother was Anu's half-sister. Anu's first born son was Enki, by Anu's official spouse, his sister. But birth from a full-sister did not qualify Enki to be the legal successor. Thus was born the on-going rift between brothers Enlil and Enki. The Anunnaki, as a race, cherished purity in their bloodlines; this belief controlled the rules of succession.

Enlil's first born son with NinMah (Enlil's half-sister) was Ninurta. Enki's first son (also with NinMah, his half-sister) was Mar.Duk, known as Ra in the land of the Great Pyramid. Mar.Duk believed his father Enki was unjustly denied the succession to the kingship of Nibiru. This was the root cause of Mar.Duk's on-going efforts to control Eridu and E.Din during the period after the Deluge.

End Note 14: 'Atlantis:' Plato reported that Solon, a priest in Egypt, told him Atlantis was 'beyond the pillars of Hercules.' Historians have placed Atlantis in the mid-Atlantic, or the Azores, or the Caribbean or under the ice of Antarctica. In 2015 a National Geographic program showed the flat delta in southwest Spain where the remains of the Atlantis harbor can be seen under the earth.

End Note 15: 'Tilmun:' When animosity threatened to lead to war between the Lords of Kien, the 'civilized' world was divided into four quarters: the desert river with the Great Pyramid called E.kur; the land between the two rivers above the Gulf; the Land of Rama in the Far East and Tilmun, the Land of Missiles, the prohibited area of the Sinai Peninsula. Tilmun was both a landing field for space vehicles and the storage field for the nuclear tipped missiles, which were called the 'Brilliance of Enlil.'

End Note 16: 'Mar.Duk:' Among the Anunnaki lords the matter of succession to the throne was a serious matter. Mar.Duk, son of Lord Enki, was fourth in line behind Lords Enlil and Enki, and Enlil's son, Ninurta. He grew up believing his father had been denied his heritage; Enki was the first born of Anu, but Enlil was the first born of Anu with Anu's half-sister Antu.

As a consequence, Mar.Duk continued to maneuver to achieve control of all of Ki.en although Lord Enlil was Lord of the Land. It is quite possible that Mar.Duk was responsible for the accidental death of Dumuzi, the Aryan beloved of Inanna. He was ordered to be shut-up in the Great Pyramid. The sisters of Mar.Duk pleaded for his release from the pyramid. They were successful. To release him a shaft was dug upward from the 'Queen's Chamber' to reach the Grand Gallery above the blocks that closed access to the 'King's Chamber.'

End Note 17: Utnapishtim (aka Noah) and the Great Flood: A monitoring station at the tip of Africa reported the three-mile-thick ice cap on the southern pole might slip into the ocean. The Titans confirmed the approach of Nibiru might cause the ice to slip. Enlil used this disaster to remove his royal relatives (and the I.gi.gi) from Earth. The royals were lifted into space; and saw the flood sweep over the land. Many of the 'gods' wept for their 'Sons and Daughters of Earth.'

Utnapishtim, father of Gilgamesh, was ruler of Shu.Rup.Pak, a 'Place of Well-Being' north of Sippar in Shin'ar. Library of Ashurbanipal tablets relate he was told by Lord Enki to build a submersible vehicle for his family and the seed of all living things.

End Note 18: Inanna/Ishtar was the granddaughter of Nin.Ti. Inanna was famous as the seducer of men; her goal was always to gain power. There is conjecture she slept with her grandfather, Lord Enki, to gain the position of goddess of Erech, Anu's temple. In later years she became mistress of Babylon while Mar.Duk ruled in Babylon. After the nuclear disaster she became a priestess at the temple of Isis, near the Great Pyramid. She was 'Goddess of War and Love.'

Nin.Ti held the title of 'Lady Life.' To the Egyptians she was Hat. hor, mistress of Ekur, the Great Pyramid. Her title was also Nin.ĥar. Sag, mistress of the Sinai Spaceport, the Restricted Zone called Tilmun.

End Note 19: 'Tilmun:' Lord Mar.Duk in Babylon refused to abandon his claim to Command of the Four Lands. The Council of Twelve, including Enlil and his father ẊAnu, voted to obliterate the Spaceport on the Sinai Peninsula. There were seven nuclear missiles available. Mount Most Supreme, the spaceport was destroyed, as were Sodom, Gomorrah, Mohenjo-Daro and Harappa, the capital city of the New Hittite Empire in the Indus Valley.

In the aftermath, the deadly black cloud came out of the Sinai and killed every living thing in seven cities in Mesopotamia. It required 70 years before these cities were again declared habitable: Ur, Eridu, Nippur, Erech (Anu's temple city), Lagash, Larsa and Babylon.

End Note 20: Tiahuanaco (also Tiwanaku): Tiahuanaco and Puma Punco ruins are south of the great Lake Titicaca in Bolivia. They were destroyed by the Great Flood which left evidence of water on their stones. In the following years survivors arrived from Atlantis and began to develop crop strains (wheat, barley, maize, radishes) in the highlands of Bolivia. Recent (2015) archaeological research seems to suggest that Tiahuanaco may have been an ore processing station.

End Note 21: 'Ekur, the Great Pyramid:' Ekur was built by Thoth/ Enoch before the global cataclysm that flooded the Mediterranean and Mesopotamia. The pyramid was built by Enoch and an unknown acoustic engineer who built the resonating chamber (using granite with silicon quartz crystals) to respond to a frequency of A 438 hertz. The five beams above the 'King's Chamber' are 'tuned' harmonic resonators. Ekur was a power plant to amplify the Earth's vibrations and (some think) to send a form of energy skyward to support the Deep Space and shuttle vehicles of the Anunnaki.

An Arab historian Al-Magrizi noted Enoch "read in the stars that the Flood was about to come. So he had the pyramids built and had hidden inside them treasures, learned writings, and all those things he feared might get lost or disappear, so that they would be protected and well preserved." (from the Khitet, written by Al-Magrizi).

Enoch, builder of the Great Pyramid, also known as Hermes (in Greek) or Idris among the Arabs, was the son of Jared, son of Mahal'aleel, the son of Ca-i'nan, the son of Enosh, the son of Seth, the son of Adam.

Some recent undersea research seems to suggest a similar pyramid continues to operate inside the Bermuda Triangle.

End Note 22: 'House of Crystal:' The Anunnaki Captain Shar is about to retire to the Bryne Valley of Ireland. This is the site where Lord Enki (or a subordinate) informed the Titans that the coming Deluge was due to their sinning with the local women. The 'Corded Ware' people (builders of New Grange) quickly abandoned their villages and moved on to the European mainland. New Grange fits the description of the House of Crystal found in the Book of Enoch.

READ MORE ABOUT IT... (A SMALL SAMPLE)

Hancock, Graham. *The Sign and the Seal.* New York, NY: Touchstone, 1992.

Hapgood, Charles H. *Earth's Shifting Crust.* New York, NY: Pantheon Books, Inc. 1958.

Josephus, Titus Flavius. (trans. by William Whiston, A.M.) *The Life & Works of Flavius Josephus.* New York: Holt, Rinehart & Winston, (no printing date). Book I: *Antiquities of the Jews.*

Lewis, L.M. *Footprints on the Sands of Time.* New York: New American Library, 1975.

Pye, Michael & Kirsten Dalley. *Lost Cities & Forgotten Civilizations.* New York: Rosen Publishing Group, 2013.

Sitchen, Zacharias. *Wars of Gods and Men.* New York: HarperCollins, 1985.

Velikovsky, Immanuel. *Worlds in Collision.* New York: The Macmillan Company, 1950.

Van Daniken, Erich. *Chariots of the Gods.* New York: Putnam & Sons, 1970 (© 1968).

Woolley, Sir Leonard. *Excavations at Ur: A Record of Twelve Years' Work.* New York: Thomas Cromwell (no pub date).

Annotated Bibliography: The annotated bibliography of 95 texts will be found in the novel *The Pilot's Mate,* also published by Create Space, available on Amazon. A flat copy of the full bibliography suitable for copying is $5 & $2 S&H from the author's website: **martyduncan.us.**

AUTHOR BIOGRAPHY

Marty Duncan, BA, MAT, EdD, served in the US Navy during the Vietnam era. He taught English and journalism before embarking on a thirty-year career as a public school superintendent.

Duncan turned to historical fiction in his early retirement. His first novel, *Gold...Then Iron* takes place in the Iron Range of Minnesota just prior to World War II. *Iron Lake Burning* relives Minnesota's longest teachers' strike, while his novel of the Dakota/Sioux war of 1862 became the trilogy *Black Powder, Gray Hope.*

Shin'ar, My Love was inspired by Von Daniken's *Chariots of the Gods* and a moment of clarity while visiting Sacsayhuaman, outside Cuzco, Peru. Duncan came to the conclusion that the Incans could not possibly have built such a monolithic structure—raising an important question: who did?

Duncan lives with his sweetheart of fifty years in southern Minnesota.

Made in the USA
Charleston, SC
15 April 2016